I0681344

DECEPTION AT GABRIEL'S TRAILS

THE COMPLETE SERIES

VOL. 2

MIRIKA MAYO CORNELIUS

author of Murders at Gabriel's Trails (VOL.1)
and Sins of Bain

of

The Gabriel's Trails book series

DECEPTION AT GABRIEL'S TRAILS: THE COMPLETE SERIES

Copyright © May - October 2016, Mirika Mayo Cornelius
An Akirim Press publishing / Book cover by Rod Cornelius
akirimpress.com   mirikacornelius.com

DECEPTION AT GABRIEL'S TRAILS: THE COMPLETE SERIES

Acknowledgements

All glory, honor, praise and total worship to God Almighty, Jesus Christ and Holy Spirit. You are my everything.

To my son, I love you. You give me motivation and inspiration.

To my husband, I love and admire you.

To my parents, I thank and love you.

To the readers of this book series and my other written works, thank you so very much.

mirikacornelius.com

DECEPTION AT GABRIEL'S TRAILS: THE COMPLETE SERIES

Table of Contents

DECEPTION AT GABRIEL'S TRAILS: THE COMPLETE SERIES

DECEPTION

AT

GABRIEL'S TRAILS

Deception at Gabriel's Trails

Two years after the Murders at Gabriel's Trails, one would think everything is solved and laid to rest. However, just when you think there is peace, Deceptions reveal themselves straight out of those same hostile streets.

At the same time Alexis reconnects with a young man from her past, a secret is uncovered that places her at odds with the same merciless gangsters that she thought she'd escaped, except now, they are much closer to her than ever before!

Two years after the
Murders at Gabriel's Trails…

He looks around the dusty area and angrily grabs the rag that hangs from his back pocket, throwing it viscously to the floor. A massive amount of heartache consumes him as he stands in the middle of a construction area where those around him are already driving away for the day, leaving him to clean up the mess left behind. Finally, he sits down on the slabs of wood and remembers the days he lost members of his family, all murdered in Gabriel's Trails.

"All because of me!" he shouts as the memories of the deceased are brandished in his head, the way they looked and even smelled the days that they died. He was only seventeen, a whole two years ago, and the murders still feel like yesterday. He's never entered Gabriel's Trails again, although he passes by it just about every day, as well as the wealthy neighborhood right outside of it that infuriates him to no end, Dominion Lakes. Before acquiring this job, he searched for a multitude of jobs that wouldn't take him near this particular area, but the only job that could spare to pay him under the table for tightening up the odds and ends around the work area is the one that is up the road from the neighborhood that destroyed his whole family.

"Hey man, you good?"

"Yeah, yeah, I'm cool. Just taking a break. Just a little tired is all," he responds to the construction worker who runs back inside to get his wallet.

"Yeah, see, this right here," the man continues after retrieving his billfold, "This is the difference between hassle and hustle. It's a hassle if my wife finds out I lost it, and I have to hustle harder because I lost what's in it," he laughs although what he said made Javis' stomach pain at the thought of the responsibilities dumped on him and only him by many terrible events that continue to happen in succession.

It was exactly one year ago that his mother became ill. The doctors couldn't find anything terribly wrong with her that would cause her health to diminish the way it had, and it was just about every week, she would pass out onto the floor wherever she was, right in the middle of whatever she was doing. The last time she passed out, it was on the living room floor, and it was his younger, sixteen year old brother Joseph who found her there still breathing but immobile. Javis was outside cutting the yard when he heard his brother hollering like a madman. It was then that Javis began to figure out exactly what was wrong with his mother, and it was the same thing that had been causing him anguish every single day since they'd abruptly fled Gabriel's Trails.

"I hear you, man, I hear you. Get home safe. Don't want your wife coming here looking for you and gettin' on me about it," Javis jokes.

"Later," the guy waves as he runs off toward his car.

Tears break free from Javis' eyes as he watches the man run quickly to get home to his family, something he and his family lost a portion of when they lived in the place that he dared to ever call his home again. Every time he thinks about Gabriel's Trails, a rush of sadness and overwhelming anger and guilt overtake him as if he still has something of which to rid himself, despite having already done enough before his escape.

As he slides himself back up the wall, wiping his tears does nothing for his emptiness inside. Not only did he lose half of his family, but all the money he'd collected from the one girl he ever cared for, the same girl who he feels is also mostly responsible for all that has transpired in his life over the last couple of years, is gone. From his mother getting sick with absolutely no medical insurance as well as buying the house, it left him a nineteen year old man with nothing but responsibility and imminent ruin in his life. Javis has nowhere to turn, so instead of taking the bus, he decides to walk home, almost hoping that a stray bullet would land him face down on the sidewalk as he passes by the neighborhood of his enemies – Gabriel's Trails.

As he passes the main entrance, every visible part of his skin rises, and he begins to perspire, breathing deeply, as he fights the urge to enter. He's never understood why on one hand he hates the area so much, but on the other hand, he feels like he has to return to the spot that started his downfall. It is on this very day that he decides to walk closer to the neighborhood than he's ever been since leaving. Finally, he crosses the street and walks inside. It's not long before his eyes are overtaken by the heap of ashes that still remain from the very day his family moved away, causing him to question how death somehow missed him, of all people, more than once…while also missing the female who started it all.

**

"I'm an adult! Get off of me!" she shouts venomously at the man standing before her whom she's lost respect for years ago ever since their confrontation in the garage when she was only sixteen years of age.

"Alexis, sit down! What has gotten into you lately?" her mother asks as her father stands idly by in the doorway that connects the kitchen to the living area, wishing he could slap her as she's been such a strain in his life.

Alexis glares at her father, and he continues to stare back at her, growing increasingly impatient with the behavior she is displaying to her mother as a result of her anger towards him. Ever since she and he shared an awesome secret between one another, their distance has grown worse. Her mother would be lying if she pretends not to notice...but she's always been great at pretending.

"I just feel like you're suffocating me," she answers, lowering her voice, realizing that lashing out at her mom would mean she's lashing out at the wrong person. "That's all it is. Since when can't I come and go as I please? I am grown now, so can't I at least do that?" she asks frustrated at her hovering parents.

"That won't be wise at all, Lorah," her father interjects. "She's only eighteen years old, and if she can reject college, then she can reject rights. It's that simple." He wipes his clean shaven face as he glances at the television. "That's all that will be said about it, isn't that right, Alexis?"

"Mom…"

"Listen to your father. He's right. You prefer to go and work at a department store," she continues, waving her hand in disgust, "over working in a position that will further your career at what you've been talking about doing all your life."

"Well I changed my mind, mom. Is that okay? I changed my own mind," she retorts, furious with her parents, but more so at the man who is responsible for half of her life. "I quit. I don't work there anymore. I'm writing." She glances at a piece of literature on the counter that her mom has been working on. "I've decided to work on launching my own magazine. I want to write, just like you."

"A magazine? Since when?"

"Since I just didn't want to tell you yet, until it was already up and running online so I can gather readers. That's when. Isn't that how it works, ma? An audience?"

Flabbergasted, her mother, an African American female author who also has her very own reputable magazine column, places her hand on her chest and turns back to see the blank expression on her husband's face. Generally, when there is something to be excited about, he usually turns red, but this time, his white skin remains very much unchanged. "Well, aren't you excited? Did you already know she wanted to be a writer and founder of her own magazine? Michael, I think that's great." She turns back to face her daughter. "That's absolutely wonderful."

"I need to leave though. I have research to do that requires much more than what these lovely, luscious walls can bring," she states, taking another jab at her father unbeknownst to her mom. "I need some experiences outside to make a magazine worth the read," she stresses. She leans in, kisses her mom on the cheek, and glares at her father who knows all she is saying is a lie. He can't question it, however, because it would be out of character for him, leading to more questions from his unsuspecting wife that he isn't prepared to answer.

"Good job," he stammers in his attempt to find words that go against his true feelings. "I had no idea…and you used to tell me everything. I suppose you can be allowed to harbor some secrets until you're ready to expose them…at the right time and all." This verbal jab wiped the sarcastic expression from Alexis' face as she turns to walk out of the house.

"See ya later."

"Bye, hon," her mom responds before turning her attention to her husband. "Did you just hear that? Looks like she won't be taking after you after all," she giggles. "My daughter, the writer." She waltzes over to him, gives him a soft, quick kiss on the lips and walks away, however, she doesn't realize that Alexis is more like her father in other ways that she would never imagine.

As the door slams behind Alexis, her father stands there in silence, cringing at the secrets they both share and his own that no one knows about at all. In less than one minute, he hears the garage door open, the car start up, and his daughter put the car in reverse. She's gone.

The streets continue to perform the task of closing in on her. Ever since the day her secret was revealed, she felt like she needed to abruptly leave her existence, never to return. Not only had she managed to live with herself after killing someone whom she thought she couldn't live without, she never got over the trouble she brought to the Moores family. They were innocent of everything, and although they equate her with evil, she never meant any of her actions to their detriment. There were far too many murders at Gabriel's Trails that year, and the root cause was her.

As she turns right at the intersection, she barrels down the road in her sports car, livid at the situation she's forced to live in. "Magazine," she sighs, shaking her head in disbelief that she placed herself into another lie that she has to somehow make good on so her parents will stay off of her back. She remembers the times when they hardly looked her way, allowing her to mostly go and come as she pleases, but ever since she forced her father's hand with a confession, causing him to give away thousands of dollars, he's convinced that now he needs a tighter leash. The problem is that dogs break their leashes all the time, and sometimes, because of that leash, they choose never to return home, taking their chances on a new life elsewhere.

Soon she approaches another light where, to her right, is the main entrance to Gabriel's Trails. She rarely looks that way anymore due to hurtful memories of losing someone she liked so much. As usual, tears begin to form at the bottom of her eyes, but before those tears fall, the light turns green, and she presses on the gas but then notices a figure walking to her right. Generally, she doesn't offer anyone a right of way, especially at the corner of the neighborhood from where all her troubles have come, but when she recognizes the person standing there on the edge of the curb, she halts her every action. Her car's windows have heavy tint, so although she stares him from his head to his feet, admiring him after a whole two years of being apart, he can't recognize her inside the vehicle as it stalls, creating a back up in traffic.

Tempted, she places her fingertip atop the window controls, and her finger trembles. Before she presses the control to roll the window down which would expose her identity, a car's horn sounds off from behind her vehicle, and she presses down on the gas, creating a screeching sound with her wheels. She doesn't go too far down the road until she turns around. By the time she looks back up, he's already jay-walking, stepping on the curb that lines the other side of the street. She waits until he will no longer be able to see her car, places on her emergency blinkers, and continues slowly down the road until he is once again in her line of vision.

By this time, he's made it all the way down the road, walking very fast, almost in stomps toward his destination. She's never seen him walk like that. Instead, according to her memory, he was always calm but confident and straight forward, and it came out in his bodily behavior. This walk was more agitated and angry, as if he was after someone or something yet to be found.

Alexis turns the car onto the same street where he walks and then looks into her rear view mirror at Gabriel's Trails. Now, she knows why he walks the way he is walking, understanding totally. She's never seen him on this path since the day he left, and the only possible explanation for this visual is that he decided to return, if but for only one time, reminding her of the day that she decided to make that same return. It always backfires.

She pulls up quickly a little ways in front of him, parks her car behind a closed down drug store on another street, and proceeds to connect with him, hesitantly but leaving herself no other option. She must go and speak to him at least once before she never gets the opportunity again.

Arriving at the street where she saw him walking, she notices that he is several feet in front of her. Her knees begin to get weak and her stomach starts to unsettle as she slows her gait in order to catch her breath. He's slightly bigger now, in the sense of a stronger build than when he was seventeen. His clothes are jagged and dirty, as if he's been working all day long in the smoldering sun.

Finally, she speeds up, hoping to catch him before he makes another turn onto a side street because she hates even walking the main road to Gabriel's Trails, although she's long figured out that nothing happens on the outside hardly, just on the inside. As he stops at the curb, awaiting traffic to come to a halt, she calls.

"Javis."

It's obvious he hears her as all his fidgeting and arm swinging comes to a halt. She watches from the back as he lifts his head high while his chest inhales so much air that his shoulders increase in mass. Alexis stops cold in her tracks when he turns around slowly with his fists clenched. His eyes lock onto hers, and with insurmountable anger, he storms toward her.

"Stop, Javis!" she panics, yet, not fleeing her position. "Javis, please," she continues to plead as overwhelming dread sends her to tears. She stands firm, prepared to take whatever power his fist throws because for the same two years, she hasn't been able to hurt herself enough in attempts to lessen her own pain and guilt. "I'm sorry! I'm so sorry, Javis, I'm begging you to let me talk!" she yells with her arms outstretched for protection.

"Let you talk for what?" he shouts, finally coming within arm's reach of her flawless skin and apologetic appeals. Standing there raging with a bruised heart in a strong body, it's evident he lacks the control over himself that he once had, and Alexis knows she's in danger. "Get the hell outta my face! When you see me, leave me," he demands loudly, causing a couple of cars who pull up on the side of the road to roll their windows down and listen.

Alexis nearly breaks down in fear of what could happen to her, but she reaches out to him anyway, touching his fist, but immediately, he swings his arm outward, forcefully shoving it away. "Javis, wait!" she calls, reaching for his arm this time, deciding that his forgiveness is worth the threat of being hit or even dying because she can't live with herself too much longer…without him. She takes hold of his wrist as tightly as she can, but when he yanks back this time, Alexis goes down to the sidewalk, having fallen over as a result of his power. Then finally she screams, "Just forgive me! Please, forgive me."

She sobs uncontrollably, her head near the curb, far too close to the road as cars are passing by as if she wants to be killed because she isn't removing herself from danger. Before Javis turns around to leave her there to drown in his consuming anger, a large truck comes barreling their way. He looks down at the girl he once cared so much about, beyond his fury, and finds the ability to lift her up before the truck creates a terrible end. When Alexis feels his hands around her arms, lifting her from the pavement, she doesn't even look into his face once she's on her feet. She only sobs, collapsing into his chest, ashamed of herself and deeply sorry for what her presence in his life has done. Javis, aware of what pain feels like, removes his protective hands from her, but continues to allow her to cry upon his chest as public eyes look on.

"It was before I met you," she begins to explain as she sits inside her car with Javis. His body reclines against the side of her car door, feeling loads of anxiety as he forces himself to hear her out. "It wasn't like I knew how much trouble I'd gotten myself into. I was stupid. I met him right outside the trails, the side that opens up to my neighborhood. He was nice to me. He even took me for a walk through the place. I was infatuated," she continues as she finally looks to her right, hoping to see into his eyes. That's only a hope, however. "He was showing me things I'd never seen before and giving me the attention I wanted…that I never had."

Javis inhales. It sickens him to hear her story, but he continues to listen to the story that he's never heard before in full. All he knows is that she was involved with a man when she wasn't even of legal age, and it is all because of that man, the worst troubles ever imagined hit his home.

"I went to see him one day, and everything I thought he was, he really wasn't. He'd hurt me so badly. I was in shock because I really did think he loved me and only me, but when I saw him with that woman…" she pauses, and clears her throat, "It doesn't matter how I felt, Javis. I accidentally shot him. I didn't mean it…"

"The hell you mean *you didn't mean it*? That's what happens when you aim a gun and your hand is on the trigger. And so this guy was a gangster…and you didn't know?" he asks in disbelief, still looking away from her. "This dude lives in the neighborhood across from you!"

"I didn't know! It's not like I could ask around, Javis," she yells, frustrated with herself. "I wasn't even supposed to be with him. It was an illegal relationship."

"Did he ever attack you?"

She falls silent.

"Did he?" he shouts. "Did he attack you first for you to have shot him?"

"No," she quickly responds.

Then, he finally turns to gaze at her in amazement. "You know, *you* sound more like the gangster to me, Alexis. Just covered up in your parent's money. You caused this. Blame it on him all you want, but it was you." After glaring at her in disgust, he opens the car door and gets out. Before he even gets his feet on the ground, she grabs him again, but this time, throwing her body over towards him in desperation. "Man, what, Alexis, what?" He pulls free and stalls, failing to see her point in wanting further conversation.

"I gave you that money! I gave it to you. I tried! I got it to you so you could move away, make a fresh start."

"You didn't give me shit! You owe my family more than that. Don't think you can validate your ties with me by some damn money. I'm not you." He pulls free and slams the door, but she exits as well, only to meet him at the back of the car.

"I didn't shoot you. I gave you all I could, even at the cost of my own life! I was willing to die to make everything right, Javis, to make everything better."

"My brother's dead! Yeah," he pauses, "He is dead, and you talk about the cost of *your* life? He was completely innocent and ended up tied up in your shit."

Alexis pauses and shakes her head, not understanding how or why his brother fits into her situation. Her mouth is gaped open, but nothing comes from it as her emotions take a turn for the worse.

"Oh," he responds, shaking his head. "You didn't know. How could you know? It wasn't on the damn news. Nothing makes it to the news with us poor people, right, Alexis? Let you die though…"

"What happened?"

"They killed him. I still don't know who did it either," he says, tossing his hands up in the air in a fit of hopelessness. "Do you? You know everything else, Lex."

"I don't know! I don't know!" She falls to the ground once again, but this time, her appearance changes to one Javis has never seen before. He catches a glimpse of it when she peers up into the blue sky, and it's the same type of lost and hopeless agony that he feels many days out of the year. It's a look that spells out giving up, and despite his anger, for the first time, he believes that maybe everything that happened may not have been planned at all. Maybe the once little naïve rich girl finally understands the trauma her lies caused and that money won't make that trauma disappear.

"Alexis," he states, subduing his anger as he kneels down to her as her hair dangles in nasty oil that's leaked from a car onto the rugged road. "Alexis," he repeats, his hand finally grazing her back with a light touch, replacing the fist that he struggled not to hit her with only less than fifteen minutes ago.

"Javis, I didn't know all this would happen. I was afraid, just afraid. I gave you the gun. It was his gun. It was his…and then I did something awful that night, something terrible, but…I felt like it was the only way to protect myself. I was trying to protect myself and have you protect yourself as well." she moans through her tears.

Immediately, Javis makes her close her mouth as he thinks about everything he's done with the gun that she'd given to him back when he lived at the Trails. If he didn't have the gun, he knows that he would have already been dead. Alexis doesn't know about the shooting nor the stabbing. No one does as far as he knows, except for those who got their revenge, and if whatever Alexis feels she was forced into doing back then, he now understood totally. Sometimes Gabriel's Trails will bring a nightmare to a person's own yard, unannounced, causing a person to fight back in the worst way.

"I understand. I understand, Alexis," he begins to sob along with her. "I understand."

They both sat there behind her car on the dirty road caring for each other like they haven't been cared for by any other person since they last looked in each other's eyes. At the same time, life still goes on in the place that left them broken – Gabriel's Trails.

**

"I already told you. I really don't want to go over there." Tryina states while gazing over the treetops beyond Gabriel's Trails in the direction of the wealthy neighborhood that she hardly ever thinks about. "They'll spot us a mile away, and you know what that means," she threatens while rolling her eyes with a not-so-nice grin.

"No, what that really means is they'll have enough sense to watch their mouths, at least until we get out of there before they start talking trash," her friend of two and a half years laughs, feeling really pressed to hang out with a new, unknown group of people. "You really haven't done much of anything since your brother passed away, Tryina. You've just gotten more and more reserved, like you're in another world. I just want you to live a bit more…instead of just going to that piece of odd end job."

"But it's *my* odd end. Forget you," she retorts, slightly offended that her friend isn't happy that she isn't making a living off the streets which was exactly what killed her brother. It's always been tempting to take over a piece of where he left off. However, she wants to believe that she's nothing like her brother, although, she secretly knows otherwise. She'd just rather keep private about herself in many ways because she's always felt determined in one direction, but held to loyalty in another. Most days, she walks around trapped as two people in one body, grateful that no one knows what goes on inside her head. "I enjoy my legal tender, so you and your sideways talk can walk, Macy."

"Stop getting so offended, damn. Listen, you come with me, just to make me feel like I'm not out of place in this big mansion, around all those rich girls. I don't know how her other friends may get down, so I need someone to help me out. You know, help me feel at home in a strange place.

How about it? Come on. I know you've never been to Dominion Lakes on invite, and if you have, why didn't you invite me?" she inquires, but Tryina only shakes her head at her pestering friend, finally giving in. Besides, Macy is the closest she has to a sister, therefore, she considers her the only bit of family she has left in the whole world. Her brother was her only family left, and before he died, he'd become her legal guardian.

"Alright. I'll go," she says, caving in to Macy's begging. "And to answer your insinuation, no, I've never been invited because we…I never was supposed to associate with them," she answers as her voice drifts off while she remembers the rules that fell over her while her older brother was alive. The rules were harsh but made to keep her safe. One wrong move outside of Gabriel's Trails would make her a potential target due to his gangster lifestyle, and Tryina never attempted to disobey, even now. Just thinking about making friends outside of Gabriel's Trails, although she's eighteen and grown, gives her the jitters. "Don't ask me not to be myself because I don't fake it for fortune or friends, Macy. That's not me, and besides that," she continues, rolling her eyes and kicking the ants off the porch that have already found something dead to nibble on, "I'm cool with being all by myself with an occasional friend that gets on my nerves," she jokes. Then, her expression changes, as if she's looking at something far away in the distance.

"You okay?"

"Yeah," she snaps, out of her daze and glances back at her well dressed friend. Macy always leaves her house looking not only respectable but like she lives nowhere around Gabriel's Trails at all. She dates a small time drug dealer who is originally from Gabriel's Trails, but he now lives on the outside in a neighborhood several blocks away. Despite that, he is always welcome to come inside after having ties to many of the people in the Trails. It's like he never moved away, but the one thing he's forbidden to do is make his money on the inside without paying his fair share. Everything else, he's welcome to doing with no problems. Besides all that, he takes care of Macy very well, but no matter how great his treatment of her is, she knows that his type of crime doesn't really pay in the long run. Therefore, this connection with a wealthy set of friends in the next neighborhood on the other side of the trails could be a slow moving but steady gold mine to real, legal money. Macy is one to repeat the saying…it's not what you know but who you know with a bunch of prestige who can open the door or help you open it. She's always wanted to be, in her words, somebody.

Tryina, on the other hand, has always known that she was somebody, with or without prestigious people around and their money. To her, all money looks green, legal or illegal. From what she learned from her brother, all of it was illegal in some way or another, and the rich have always had their stake in the crime but never wants the poor to get in on the deal. At least that was his reason for validating his way of life.

"So it's a go?" Macy asks with the excitement of a school girl, although she graduated last year.

"Yeah, Macy. I'm gettin' ready to go back inside, so meet me up at trail number 2."

"We're walking?"

"Yeah. I'm not driving, and you aren't either."

"Why not?"

"Guess, Macy?" Tryina laughs while shaking her head in disbelief. Macy thinks about it for only a second, and

27

then understands Tryina totally. Even though they are crime free, the people in their lives aren't, and because Macy just met this rich girl not too long ago, she can't be trusted. No one outside of the trails can be trusted, and if anyone brings in trouble, they are held accountable. It's how it's always been.

"My mistake," she smiles. "I know," she sighs.

"At what say...eight o'clock we meet?"

"That'll work," her friend responds, spinning around to head back to her home which is only three blocks further into the neighborhood.

"See you then, Macy." Tryina doesn't wait for another word from her friend as she jumps up from the porch, twists around on one foot and enters her home, the one she shares with no one anymore. When she shuts the door, there's a mirror hanging directly in front of her that she stares into at her reflection. "Come on, Tryina," she whispers. "Get it together. You have to." Then she glances down at her brother's obituary, full of guilt, and then continues to encourage herself. "Either live or die, just like him."

Eight o'clock comes around fast, and Tryina is within eyesight of Macy who stands at the beginning of trail number two wearing red shorts and a white top that's tied in the front to appear almost preppy. This is the absolute opposite of Tryina's look who is wearing long braids that stretch down over her skin tight, black shirt and stretch jeans that are decorated with slits all the way down both thighs while black wedges cradle her feet.

"What is taking you so long? Get a move on with those high ass shoes," Macy grins.

"Well, I see you're ready to sip tea and look like the American flag, aren't you?" Tryina jokes as she admires her friend's suburban appearance. Macy even went as far as putting her hair in a neat bun while wearing a pair of small, pearl earrings. The closer Tryina gets, the more she laughs. "Really, Macy?"

"Shut up, and come on," she responds, sticking her neck out and grabbing her friend by the arm. "Keep your jokes to yourself until we're back in the Trails. I know I look like an uptight, hot mess."

They both laugh and head out of Gabriel's Trails and into another world that neither one of them is truly prepared to enter. By the time they reach the end of the trail, the huge homes are already within full view in the setting sun. It's a brand new adventure for these two young ladies as this is their first time ever walking through such an affluent row of homes, despite the fact that Gabriel's Trails is truly a next door neighbor. Most people leave from the front, or main entrance, of Gabriel's Trails in order to feel more secure about their surroundings and not like they are being watched.

"I already feel the eyes. They're watching," Tryina states as she tugs on her shirt slightly, feeling anxious about the whole trek into waters that she feels she's already drowning in.

"Stop tugging," she snaps, slapping her friend's hand down from her shirt. "If someone is watching, give them something good to see."

"I don't know about this. My brother always said…"

Macy stops, only to walk directly in front of Tryina who stares right back at her, ready to turn back around to find lodging in the place she's known as her protection since she was a child. "What is your problem, Tryina? You never act like this. Why are you so jumpy all of a sudden? It's just a damn neighborhood. You make me think something else is up that I don't know anything about. Is there?" Macy asks, poking her face nose to nose with her hesitating friend. "I know something's up."

Tryina wants to speak but doesn't because the truth is that she is trying to hide something, but that's never for Macy to know…ever. She only shoves the night her brother died to the back of her mind and pretends she never knew the details about it, then responds hastily to her friend who is standing there encouraging her to speak up by placing her hands on her hips and stretching her eyeballs to every end.

"The only thing that's up is that I don't like being here. This isn't us."

"It will be. It will be soon enough. More than likely, this batch of ladies will have some men you can case. Get yourself a man while I get my career by hobnobbing."

"I'll take the career path first, just like you, Macy, just in case my man leaves or dies."

Macy silences as she feels the tension and sadness in Tryina's tone. Therefore, she decides to keep walking, leaving Tryina to walk beside her sorting out her emotions. As they reach three streets into the neighborhood with its plush lawns, sprinkler systems, and electric fences with dogs running right up to them, causing both Tryina and Macy to make mad dashes in confusion as to why the dogs stop attacking, they finally reach the home to which they're invited.

"I hope no one was looking," Tryina pants as she grabs her braids and tosses them to her other shoulder.

"Did you see that damn dog?"

"We saw the same exact thing, Macy," she grins, "But we didn't see that invisible ass fence either."

"Got my hair all messed up probably," she complains as they walk toward the driveway. "Do I still look…"

"Yeah, you look fine," Tryina responds as she takes in the huge home that she's about to enter. She can feel the nervousness take over her body, and as she tries to conceal her anxiety, Macy skips to the door and rings the bell. This causes Tryina to slow her gait to a near halt until someone answers the door. All her life, the trails forbade her from this area, and now it feels like she's in a brand new world.

It's an African American young lady who looks like she is Tryina's age of eighteen. As Tryina approaches the door, she becomes aware that the female who invited Macy had no idea she would be bringing a tag along.

"Oh, this is Tryina. You don't mind, do you, that I brought my best friend?" Macy asks, countering the odd glance Zeena gives her guest.

Tryina only stands there, listening to all the other females that sound like they are only a few feet behind the doorway. She's so apprehensive that she almost forgets to smile and respond to the female's greeting.

"No no, not at all, Macy," she stammers. "Hi, I'm Zeena. Zeena Castles," she states with her hand out in a formal greeting to a Tryina who has to prompt herself out of defense mode in order to speak back.

"I'm sorry. Hi, Tryina," she responds, failing to give her last name. It's something that she's also learned never to do, and it's not an easy habit to break. Since the gangsters she knows use it for leverage, it's the last thing she wants to divulge.

"Nice to meet you. Come on inside. We're in the entertainment room. Go on in. I'll be right there. Follow the noise," Zeena laughs without a care in the world. "We got drinks, snacks, and more food is on the way. Waiting on some more people to come over."

As Tryina walks inside, she notices how uninterested Zeena is in locking the front door, which is odd on her side of the tracks. Macy goes with the flow and glides right on down the hallway, flicking her fingers to force Tryina to follow. Turning to look back at the front door, she takes a deep breath as she listens to Zeena hum a tune inside another room. Suddenly, she feels a tug at her shirt.

"Tryina," Macy stresses between her teeth. "I just peeped in. These people ain't nobody that we need to be on our guard about. Loosen up. You're acting like someone is after you around here." She pulls her by her hand. "Don't be so embarrassing!"

Tryina's heart pumps faster, and her thoughts are racing a mile a minute as she continues to dwell and suffer in the silence that's about to erupt loudly any minute if she turns the corner to, for the first time, meet a girl…the rich girl… that she never thought she would ever encounter. They've never crossed paths, but the word in the trails among her brother's crowd is that she's still out here, and it's not over.

"Leave me alone, Macy." Tryina looks coldly at Macy, and immediately, Macy drops her hand, terrified of what she may have inadvertently stepped into when she thinks about the things she doesn't know about her friend. Macy then turns to the room full of girls, and then back at Tryina, tying the room full of girls to the hesitation of her friend.

Tryina only stares back at Macy for a couple of seconds, notices a guest bathroom to her left, and then, bolts inside. The door slams and locks, causing the girls and Zeena to flock from where they were, questioning Macy about what is going on. Macy plays it off by smiling, facing Zeena and saying, "She's not feeling too good. Vertigo. Sorry about the door." As the ladies go back down into the entertainment room, Macy glances back at the bathroom. Her stomach begins to knot up because she knows something isn't right. Meanwhile, from behind the bathroom door, Tryina is sitting on the lid of the toilet, squeezing her fists together, funneling her fury into a calmer place, just in case she hears a name she just simply can't ignore.

**

"Alexis, stop the car right here." They are on the corner, just down the road from where he lives, in a small home that they can see from where they are.

"That's where you live?"

"Yeah, for now." He looks away from her, still uncomfortable with the way he feels toward her. They share so much good and bad situations together that it's impossible to allow their conversation to go on. He believes that it's best to pretend that today never happened. "Act like we never saw each other, Alexis."

"Javis…"

"Don't push this issue. Things won't work," he looks back into her teary eyes. "They never did work. We have too much between us that…"

"But we can be together now. We're adults."

"We couldn't be together then, Alexis," he strains, feeling compassion for the state of her emotions because he's arrived at that same place, having to hold everything inside until finally realizing that the one with whom he is most angry is the same one whom he is most in need of more than ever. "But your past, and now my past, won't allow it. It won't work. We've done too much."

"I need you, Javis." Her hand moves from the gear and slowly onto his hand, her fingers sliding into his. Tears begin to fall once again as she pleads in silence, awaiting him to give her any sign that he is at least willing to try. "If I could take it all back, I would gladly take death…" It is only then that Javis allows his fingers to move over hers and hold them gently.

"We both would. I've thought about it. You know, like if I couldn't be there to take the bullets, I could join them," he starts to cry, choking back as best he can the pain and memories of his loss. "There was no way of knowing. There was no way of knowing what would happen back then, but it did." He gently lets go of her hand and exits the vehicle, only to find Alexis exiting the car as well and running to say goodbye. She stops just short, only inches, from his body, and as their eyes meet, nothing else matters. He leans in to her sadness and kisses her ever so gently on the lips, a kiss he's needed for a long time, and it's a passion that Alexis has desired since the time he left her life.

For the first time, Javis' emotions begin to unlock, having been shut up for about two years in order to become the man of a household he didn't create but needed to sustain. However, as he kisses her, she pulls back with a request.

"Will you come with me? Just for tonight?"

"I can't go anywhere with you, Alexis. Life isn't as easy for me as it is for you, so stop acting like…"

"Okay, I'm sorry," she apologizes quickly. "Will you call me?" she asks desperately. "Do that for me…for us. Will you do that for us. I don't have to see you if that's what you want, but I need to talk to you. I got no one, Javis."

He looks away at his house and then back at her. "What's the number? I'll remember."

Alexis gives him her cell phone number, and before she leaves, she gives him a kiss on his cheek, touches his fingertips and heads off. He watches as her car goes down the road, and as he dutifully memorizes her cell phone number while walking towards his house, he's startled when he spots someone staring at him through the screen door.

**

Tryina places her hand on the bathroom door's handle and slowly opens it after pacing back and forth in the wide space. She hears the stories, the many stories that continue passing from ear to ear on the streets of Gabriel's Trails, but only one story was the truth. It all started with a girl, and it is that girl, through Tryina's imagination, that she'd grown to hate, the same way her brother had grown to hate her before his death. Tryina's life was starting to come together back then, with a newfound happiness and a boyfriend she adored, until it was all taken from her…behind one little rich girl who lives in Dominion Lakes.

Finally, she steps out, able to shove her emotions to a place of control before she waltzes into the room with Macy, who waits on her at the door. Tryina's face startles Macy because it is far more enthused about the small party than it was just moments ago. Tryina notices Macy giving her a stare down on the walk down the small staircase to meet everyone, but then Macy lets out a sigh of relief, revealing that she's very happy with whatever caused her friend to lighten up while in the bathroom.

She whispers, "You on drugs?" before her feet hit the cream carpeting that covers the floor to the entertainment room.

Tryina smiles while bringing her best forward for all the young ladies to capture in order for them to feel most comfortable around her. She inspects all of them, including Zeena, as she and Macy sit beside each other on broad back, wicker chairs. Suddenly, Zeena turns the music down via remote control and locks the French doors that lead to the outside swimming pool.

"Now listen up," she states, stopping at the coffee table to pour another alcoholic drink in her wine glass.

"Why did you lock the door?" asks another guest, curious to what all the secrecy is about.

"So nobody else will just walk in, that's why!" Zeena snaps with a tipsy grin on her face. "I have something to tell you all, and I've been keeping it secret for a long damn time. You know a party isn't a party until somebody lets something out of the bag!"

"This game again, Zeena?"

"Girl, it's fun. Look, all of you take a drink. Take one or two back. I'm going first. This has to be real shit now, so spill it." She chugs down whatever is in her glass while everyone waits, and then she speaks after pushing her long, dark hair to the back of her sleeveless blouse. "I saw a murder."

"What?" a female yells out in disbelief, but Zeena quickly snaps back.

"Be quiet. You know the rules, but in case you don't…nobody talks during the confessions and secrets." She rolls her eyes like an immature girl, and continues telling her secret. "Like I said, I saw a murder, and it happened out there at those trails."

Macy feels the tension in the air grow from Tryina who sits there, her smile turned expressionless, as the words *murder* and *trails* come out of Zeena's mouth. Because she's trying to make a great first impression, she doesn't move or make a sound due to the rules of the game, but she's terrified of what Zeena may say next that could trigger who knows what from Tryina, especially if that murder has to do with her deceased brother. Although she feels the tension brewing, when she sneaks a peek at Tryina, her friend is sitting there appearing more relaxed than before. However, before she turns back to look at Zeena, she notices the movement of Tryina's fingers. They're shaking, and it's not seconds later that she places them in between her thighs and crosses her legs while she waits on the continuation of the story.

"It was a couple years back, out there in the dead of night. I just happened to be driving by one of the houses," she continues, puffing on a cigarette that she quickly puts out and fans. "One of those houses up there in the front, and I saw something that didn't look right. I kept driving though, but when I got closer to my street, I turned back around. Something just didn't feel right." She sits up in the chair, her back up straight as she pours more alcohol. "I turned my car lights off and drove back up slowly, then I kinda parked my car on the side of the road like it was there on a visit." She takes a small sip of her drink as she looks at the French doors, then back at her guests who sit there quietly waiting on the rest of the confession.

"Anyway, after I parked, I walked up close to some bushes…there used to be bushes when you walk up the sidewalk, and if you sit behind them, you can see the trails and that first street into Dominion Lakes really well and at the same time."

"Yeah they cut those down…"

"Shut up, dang!"

"Sorry," the female laughs, picking up her glass while placing a finger over her lips signifying that she won't interrupt again.

"I saw this girl pull what looked like a body from the ground. I wasn't sure because the garage door light went off, but it looked odd, so I waited. I even turned on my cell phone camera to take pictures, but it was too dark. Next thing I know, I watch as this girl drives to the trails…and I mean she drove right beside me! I thought I would have shit all in my pants, ladies. Then, she stopped the car like right there! She was right there at the trails, and my damn phone wouldn't take the pictures. So there I sat, and I saw her ass," she says, her voice transforming into something demented, as she stares off like she's witnessing it again before her very eyes. "Yeah, it was her…and there was a lady leaned back in the car seat, not even moving. Her head was just lying there, limp. That's when the killer's ass ran out of that damn driver's side door." Zeena's eyes turn back to meet the attention of every female in the room. "She ran her ass back home, and I was the one that called the ambulance later on. I had to make sure though…and I made sure I saw what I saw, too. Believe you me, I made certain."

"You said you called the ambulance. Did you call the cops?"

"Nope. The emergency personnel did...obviously. But if you're thinking I did, I didn't. I only called for the body and claimed I didn't see who attacked her when I spoke to 911. I hung up. I didn't turn her in, but I know who she is. I know *exactly* who did it."

There's a knock on the French door. Everyone looks up, and there's another young lady standing there, waiting to come in. Zeena smiles, looks back at the others, then stands as if she was never talking about anything at all, but before she opens the door, she turns around and says, "Bingo!" As she turns back around with the unlocking of the door, she faces the young lady who has about four pizzas in her hand. "Hey, Alexis. Glad you made it." She then turns toward her other guests who sit there amazed at Zeena's insinuation. "And you brought the pizza!"

**

He sets the timer for five minutes and then steps inside the shower. The water isn't even hot yet, but he can't afford to let it run without it hitting his skin. That would be a waste. Watching the dirt fall off of him from a hard day's work, he tries to relax his body while the soap does its job.

Rehearsing Alexis' telephone number in his head is like a dream and a nightmare combined, he honestly thought he would never see her again, and there were no parts of him that yearned for her until today. He turns, allowing the warmer water to soothe his back while through the thin shower curtain, he eyeballs the loose dollar bills he has that hang from his pants pocket on the floor. It's only enough to pay a partial light bill.

At the sight of the money, he closes his eyes, and decides to mentally escape now that he finally has someone to think about and possibly even talk to that knows all about what he's feeling and some of the things he's done. Alexis happens to be his nemesis, but he finds himself needing her in more ways than he could have ever dreamed. As he stands there in the shower, allowing all of the soap to rinse off of his body, the timer goes off, and he steps out onto a fancy rug that they bought after purchasing the house. By coming inside when they first moved in, no one would ever believe that they were having hard times. Everything in the house was decorated, but now, it's minus many things that he had to sell since his mother got ill. The money that he had just didn't go a long way, not as far as it could have.

"Javis!"

Immediately, Javis throws a towel around his waist and darts from the bathroom at the call of his mother. She's continuously calling his name frantically, and when he finally enters the living room, she's on the sofa with her eyes closed screaming his name but not looking at him.

"Mama! Mama, it's me. It's me, look...look!" he shouts grabbing her by her shoulders and forcing her to look in his direction. "I'm right here. It's a dream."

"No, baby, no! Where's Joseph? You see him. He was right there. He was right there," she shouts, lunging at the other chair that sits opposite where she is.

"Joseph? Ma, he's around here somewhere. Hey! Joseph!" Javis hollers as he holds his mother still. "Mama, chill! He's fine."

"You're supposed to protect him, Javis. Please, baby, don't let nothing happen to him, please!" she continues,

40

gripping her oldest son's muscular arm and holding it tightly. "I can't fight like I used to fight…"

"Joseph!" His voice barrels through the house and the brick walls as if he is a giant. "Joseph!" he calls once again before his brother rushes back inside the house as fast as he can with his cane.

"What, man, what? I went outside for a minute, just one minute and what…is mom alright?" He tosses his cane to the side and grips the chair to fall right next to her. "Ma, it's me. It's me. I'm right here. You have to calm down."

"I got my two sons. You both are here with me, right?"

"Joseph, call the hospital."

"The hospital? We don't have the money for the…"

"Just do it, man. I can't work and watch mom. Pretty soon, you have to get some work, too. Then what? Call the hospital." He then looks away from Joseph in deep thought.

"What?" his younger brother asks as he notices his short gaze.

"I'll get the money. Just call them. Tell them to come pick her up. I don't want her to have another near heart attack. I'll pack her stuff."

"You sure about this, man?"

"Bro, what else can I do? We're broke! Mama can't even work anymore. I'm damn nineteen years old with no experience doing anything but labor! We made good on the money before. They don't know we can't pay now, so while we have credit and their trust, I need to get her care…at least until I secure more money."

"I can…" Joseph starts, but Javis cuts him off.

"You can watch out for mom at the hospital after school. She needs to constantly see us, at least one of us. I'll work this out," he responds, kissing his mother on the cheek before walking back down the short hallway to get dressed. "Just do what I say, alright?" Just as he enters his room, he takes out a pen and a piece of notebook paper and writes.

**

"My favorite. Glad I came," she says as she takes a bite of the pizza that's overloaded with cheese, meat and mushrooms. "So, you live out here as well?"

"Yeah, sure do. Just right down the road," she sighs as she pulls out a paper plate and sits about five slices of pizza on it, giving a side smile. "Hi," she says dusting off her hands by clapping them together. "I'm Alexis, just in case you didn't get it back at the door. I haven't seen you in this area though…"

"No, no I'm not from around here," she responds while rubbing her fingers across the marble countertop. She's never seen one before and finds herself adoring it in many ways. "My name's Tryina. I'm just tagging along with my friend Macy who was invited here by Zeena. Been out here your whole life?"

"Not quite, but long enough to call it my first home. My family left to settle here from a neighborhood across town." Finally, she finishes grabbing her wings, fries and pizza onto a plate. "You ready?" she asks about to walk down the staircase from the kitchen as they are the last ones to prepare their plates.

"Yeah, let's go," Tryina sighs as she follows the female down the stairs. She replays everything Zeena said about the young lady in her mind and tried to imagine a girl who appears so harmless, beautiful, and fragile killing someone. She couldn't. Finally she takes her seat next to Macy once again who is eating the food like it's beneath her, tearing off pieces and sticking it in her mouth instead of picking up the whole slice and shoving it down her throat like she does outside of the presence those she's trying to impress.

"So what did I miss?" Alexis asks sitting down on the floor with her legs crossed and her plate front and center as she digs in. The first slice she picks up is so hot that the thick cheese weighs the hand tossed crust down, and she catches drooping layers with her mouth while waiting on someone to answer her question. It becomes obvious that she has no idea that she is the star of the most lethal secret in this circle of associates and friends.

"We were just playing drink and tell. You know that game, right, Alexis?" Zeena chimes in while she watches Alexis quickly look down at her plate.

"Yeah, yeah…I know that game."

"You got next?"

"No." She abruptly glances up at Zeena after catching her slick tongued remark towards her. "No, I don't *got* next. I never *got* any secrets to tell…and you know that." She then glances at everyone in the room, realizing that she's made most, if not all, of them uncomfortable with her retort.

"I agree with that. A secret is a secret right. They aren't meant to tell."

Alexis immediately shoots her attention at the girl she just met in the kitchen who is agreeing with her. "Exactly, Tryina. Exactly."

Macy quickly flashes a huge smile brought on by her nerves being shot as a result of Tryina's challenge of Zeena's party games. "Girl, you are too much," she laughs, but no one hears the joke. "There's nothing wrong with the game, though. It's just a game," she says to smooth things over.

"No, Macy." Suddenly, Tryina sends a harsh stare at Zeena while answering Macy. "Everything isn't a game." Then, she turns to face her friend who is growing more embarrassed by the second. "A secret is a secret." As she picks up her pizza, she continues. "Just like a snitch is a snitch." She takes a bite, and it isn't but two hours later that the small gathering is over, going downhill for Zeena she is disrespected by a guest she didn't even invite. The rest of the night goes by without Macy speaking another word to Tryina. Instead, she, like the rest of the girls, prepare to leave, and she exits without Tryina.

Alexis watches from the kitchen as Tryina stands there watching Macy storm out of the front door. Then, she quickly walks over, appreciative of how Tryina came to her aid and asks, "Need a lift back home or did you drive? Thanks for backing me up back there. Hardly no one ever takes on Zeena. She's cool, although sometimes she can be a nuisance."

"No," Tryina stalls, surprised that Alexis offered to drive her back home, but quickly realizing that she has no idea where her home is located. "No, I didn't drive, so…she's probably going to make me walk back," she answers deceptively.

"You got my back, then I got yours. Hold up a minute, and let me use the bathroom. I parked out back. Meet me there, and we'll head out." Then she whispers. "Don't let Zeena get to you." She smiles and walks toward the bathroom. When she hears the door shut, Tryina calmly walks back by the other young ladies and stands next to the French doors. She peers outside, and sure enough, to the right, there are two cars there on the enlongated driveway. As she stands there, she attempts to count the minutes it will take Macy to run through the trails. There's no way she's going to walk although she's perfectly safe since she's Tryina's friend. Her brother's friends own those trails now, and they're always there watching. The only people unsafe are the ones who have no business there at all. Gabriel's Trails keeps tabs on everyone and everything going on inside it.

"So, you didn't too much care for my party, I see?" the host addresses Tryina as she removes her phone from her ear and tosses it onto the loveseat.

Tryina turns to face her, unfazed by the confrontation as she has other things on her mind. "No, your party was fine. It's the game that crosses the line, don't you think so? Where I'm from, that game would never be an option."

"Haven't you ever heard of moving on in life, Tryina? Sometimes you have to abandon your old life and learn new tricks." She pauses as she searches for a flinch from Tryina, and when she doesn't see one, she continues, realizing quickly that she can't play the same mental games with her that she plays with the other girls of her circle. "No worries though. I'm not offended. We are from two totally different worlds. I may have to learn your language."

"It's the same language. I understand you perfectly...Zeena, right?"

"Yeah, Zeena."

Tryina looks up and sees Alexis walking her way. "Well, Zeena, I don't need your advice. I live in the real world."

"You ready to go?" Alexis asks as she whisks past Zeena who stands there with her arms folded and head cocked to the side with a huge grin on her face, watching Alexis walk by.

"Friends already, I see."

"Thanks for the party. It was…short." Alexis jabs before heading outside. Tryina follows.

"Well, get back home safely," Zeena grins even more, figuring out that Alexis has no idea that she's headed into Gabriel's Trails.

As she unlocks her car doors, she watches Tryina step inside her vehicle, and the girls clamor to the door like fire ants on a fallen ant bed. Feeling confident about her exit, she waves her fingers in the air at what she considers their fake smiles, sits in the car, and heads off.

"I never did like those girls that much though." She pulls off of the driveway and heads toward the neighborhood's entrance.

"So why do you even bother?" Tryina asks, searching for Macy anywhere in sight as they approach the first street in Dominion Lakes which is adjacent to the trails of Gabriel's Trails.

"Force of habit, I suppose. It's great to have someone who thinks like I think about the situation though. I could tell that you would rather be somewhere else other than with them."

"Possibly," Tryina states before noticing her point at a home to her left.

"That's my humble abode."

"Humble?"

Alexis laughs. "It looks fantastic from the outside, doesn't it?" she asks as she pulls up to the stop sign. "Which way?"

"Right. Turn right." After speaking there's a silence that Tryina must break, so she does in her own way. "So you killed someone?"

"What?" Alexis responds, shaken and nearly thrown off the road by the question. She grabs the steering wheel and pulls it quickly back onto her side of the street as Tryina continues to stare forward as if the question she asked was one of normalcy. Alexis' breathing becomes harsh and uncontrollable, however, she breaks the speed of the car and asks, "Who told you something like that?"

"Zeena,"Tryina responds after about three seconds go by. "You can turn right at the intersection again," she continues with directions. "When you came in with the pizza, she didn't mention your name but…"

"Which way?" Alexis interjects, fuming without a way to release her rage, as Tryina notices that the wealthy female didn't even hear the directions she gave, possibly due to her being engulfed in a truth that was never supposed to be revealed.

"Make another right at the light." She then turns to a frustrated appearing Alexis, her light brown skin turning a whole other shade as she makes a right turn. "I already said that. Didn't you hear me?" Tryina's voice bounces off of every window of the vehicle but doesn't land onto Alexis' ears until she says one last thing. All of the anger that she withheld while inside the magnificent home in Dominion Lakes releases itself into a controlled vibration at the back of her throat. As she remembers her deceased brother and the relationship she lost while her life was turned upside down in a matter of hours, Tryina unbuckles her seatbelt, turns to face her directly and speaks, "Turn into Gabriel's Trails…*again*."

In horror, Alexis shifts her eyes only to look back into Tryina's scorning gaze which sends her into a fight for her life. "Shit!"

Tryina grabs the steering wheel and yanks the car off the road and into the Gabriel's Trails main entrance while Alexis screams for help, slamming on the brakes. Cars beep their horns at what looks to be a wreck about to happen until they see two women attacking one another in the car. Onlookers who live at the main entrance of Gabriel's Trails run down to observe the commotion under the night sky while children who are out late, stare and point their fingers at the passenger side door flying open.

"Get your ass out!"

"Let go of me!" Alexis kicks and screams, shoving her gear in park while bracing herself on the emergency brake, fearing being pulled out of the car by her hair which Tryina is tugging on.

"All this shit happened because of you!" she fires at her, not able to shake the allegiance to her neighborhood or to her deceased brother, behaving as if she is a full blown gangster herself. "You live by the laws of Gabriel's Trails, then you die by us, too!" Tryina's rage sends a jolt of energy toward Alexis in the form of a fist to the side of her face. At the throw of Tryina's punch, Alexis is able to put a strong grip onto her wrist, pulling her a very small distance back inside the car. She takes the car out of gear and shoves down on the gas while still leaning over attempting to free her hair from Tryina's grasp. The car rolls forward quickly and Tryina finally lets go, kicking the car as she watches Alexis sit back up in a frenzy, take control of the vehicle and drive away...just as her phone rings.

Tryina answers, trembling and turning to face the crowd of people around her. "Hello?"

A male's voice answers. "I'm on my way."

**

"Why did you want me to come all the way back over here, Zeena? It's late, and I have to get back through the trails. I'm sorry about tonight, but I really have to leave," Macy apologizes as she checks the time on her cell phone. It's already nearly eleven o'clock, and as she stares anxiously behind her into the darkness of the trails, her new, wealthy friend starts speaking again.

"Just come here. Hop inside. This is gonna be really quick, and I promise you I'll take you back myself."

Hesitantly, Macy agrees, takes one more look at what time it is on her phone and then hops inside the car after looking further up the street. "You know you probably don't want to just sit here too long."

"Hell with that. I'm fine." She then reclines in the driver's seat and grins. "I know I am. Not a damn thing is gonna happen to me."

"Really?" Macy asks, totally confused about why she believes that hanging out at the trails is so safe for her as she sits inside her luxury, four door car. "Do you know something about Gabriel's Trails that I don't know because as far as what I do know since I actually live in there, *I'm* much safer on foot than you are in this car right now. As a matter of fact, if I step out, you're on your own."

"You think so, huh?" she asks, rubbing her index finger over the bedazzled steering wheel cover.

"I know so," Macy laughs as she peers through the window into the darkness, not believing how insane Zeena is behaving at the moment, as if she has power beyond a bullet. "I think you may have had a little too much to drink. Shit starts out here, and you're just a bit too close." Macy continues to stare at the street, searching for any sign of the friend she brought with her.

"You didn't see your little friend as you were coming back up the trail to meet me, did you? Is that who you're looking for out of my window by any wild chance?"

Macy turns to face her, slightly annoyed by the sarcasm in her voice. It's true. That is who she's looking for, but she lies. "No…but why would I? There are three other trails besides the one I took. She could have taken a different route easily." She then sighs in an attempt to appear calm when in reality, something is going terribly wrong, and she knows it.

"That's because she got a ride back."

"With who?" Macy leans onto the passenger side door, cocking her head to the side as she stares at Zeena, awaiting an answer. From what she knows, absolutely no one from Dominion Lakes comes through Gabriel's Trails voluntarily, hardly ever.

"That bitch ass murderer, that's who. I hate that damn girl."

Macy sits up from her seat and leans against the dashboard, altering the preppy routine she started with into more a prepped and ready-for-anything posture. Her voice even changes as she examines the way Zeena is bouncing her leg up and down in a fit and rubbing her thumb across the screen of her cell phone. "What the hell you got against her? She didn't murder your ass...now did she?" When she gets no answer from Zeena, she turns to face the trails, contemplating getting out of the car, but then she turns back around to face the tense driver. Then, she looks back at the cell phone that's still in her hand, trying to figure out what's about to happen. "Snitching isn't what we do around here, and I'm not for it. We handle everything on our own because the police won't ever do it..."

Zeena throws her head back like a wild woman against the headrest of her seat and shoves the cell phone up against the steering wheel. "Yeah, I'm snitching alright." She starts to dial, and with each number pressed, Macy feels compelled to run, but she doesn't. Instead, everything around her silences while she watches Zeena push the final button – speaker. As Zeena glances Macy's way with a demented smile, the other line picks up. Macy's breathing stops as she waits on the person on the other line to answer. It only rings once.

"Yeah, baby?" the male on the other end of the phone answers. The voice is extremely familiar to Macy, one that is mostly known by everyone in Gabriel's Trails, and if someone doesn't know it, they'll soon find out. It's a voice that's killed more than two hands can count and two feet can escape. It's someone she's already crossed, but he just hasn't discovered it yet.

"Hey. She's already gone with this little bitch I just met, to take her home named Tryina."

Within the same second that Zeena utters Tryina's name, Macy lunges forward, attacking Zeena in the face multiple times with a closed fist directly to her mouth. Blood begins to ooze everywhere, and just as the phone falls from Zeena's hand, Macy rushes to hang it up.

"Dammit!" She shoves Zeena's phone in her pocket and takes off running through the trails, and only stops one time before entering to make a desperate phone call. "Come on, come on pick up! These stupid rich ass girls!" she complains furiously as she searches around herself, ensuring that no one is too close before she runs to hide behind a tree. A male answers the phone.

"What's up?"

"Baby, get out," she weeps, the tears already rolling to her chin as she peeps back around the tree to watch Zeena wiping her face and starting up the car. "Baby, please, get out of the house. Do it now! Tryina's not with me. She's already in Gabriel's Trails, and it's Chief. He's about to meet her at the house. She got a ride back with somebody, some girl, he's about to hit. Just get the fuck out!" Before he responds, she makes a run for it, not back to Tryina's house, but to her own, except this time, she isn't confident. She's scared to death.

**

"That stupid ghetto ass...wannabe ass..." Zeena hollers as she makes her way back into her parent's mansion.

52

"My lip is mangled to all hell, and she took my freaking phone!" She bursts through the front door in serious pain as her entire bottom lip is split in the middle while her top lip suffers from a huge gash. Directly into the guest bathroom she goes as the blood gushes down her face and drips to the shiny floor beneath her feet. "I can't believe she fuckin' hit me…and for what?" she yells, rolling her eyes in disbelief, not able to digest that her plans of impressing Chief by delivering his enemy directly to him are foiled and has backfired in such a way. "I mean, damn. I had her ass, but he heard me. I know he did. He'll get her ass back because he knows exactly where her ass will be…with that fuckin' girl named Tryina," she continues, stretching her cheeks to get a better view of the splits that are destroying her mouth. "My fuckin' face!" Each time she speaks, blood oozes from the wounds. "I don't even have a phone to call the damn hospital or the damn cops!"

She storms out of the bathroom and into the kitchen where she busts open a brand new pack of dish rags, runs them under cold water, and then soaks her lips. The pain gets worse with each minute that goes by, so she decides to drive herself to the hospital. She dropped the keys back in the foyer, so as she makes her way back to the front door, her head is grabbed from behind and slammed into the opposite wall with so much force until she can't see straight. She struggles to get loose from her attacker's grip, gasping for air and footing, but she does all this to no avail as she watches herself scrape to survive. She never sees her attacker nor can she fight back against the brutality and strength of the predator behind her, slinging her by her hair. Finally, for once second, she's capable of bracing herself on the floor with the palms of her hands. However, as she tries to push herself back up to a stance to turn around, her head is drawn back by a cord around her neck, only getting a small glimpse of the person whom she never thought would come back to kill her.

Zeena stretches her arms out, reaching for the front door that is only a short distance away, however, the strength of the person behind her is so unbreakable that her body finally goes limp, and the door fades away. When there is no more movement left, after a whole minute goes by, the killer removes the cord from her throat. It's an electric cord. Zeena's head falls to the floor while the killer runs into the other room and reattaches the cord to a laptop computer that sits on the edge of a coffee table. Finally, the intruder leaves, careful to leave the front door cracked open.

Walking as calmly as possible, the attacker goes down the street with senses on high alert. Focusing on a small pebble on the concrete, she kicks it down the road as her stomach starts to quake viciously, however, she doesn't stop walking and kicking that pebble until she arrives at her house. She stalls as she notices her parents are at home, so she enters, not through the way she normally does which is through the garage. Instead, she uses the front door.

As she opens the door, there's no evident noise, so she walks calmly up the staircase, and when she finally reaches her room, she collapses against the wall. She raises her hands and there's blood all on her fingers, but she's not cut. It's from her victim, and just the sight of it makes her tremble and her mind race.

"I didn't do this," she groans silently, pushing back the fear that overwhelms her. "All this blood," she says, thrusting herself from the wall and rushing to her bathroom to cleanse her hands. As she washes, she listens for her parents who she expects any moment because when she came back into Dominion Lakes, she parked her car in the garage, then left out back to head to Zeena's house in the middle of the night. She suspects that they've already called for her since they arrived home after she left.

After she cleans off, she sits on the bathroom floor still shaking from the murder, wondering if whoever beat Zeena up was still around there, watching her choke the life from her. Her cell phone rings. Terrified at the sound, she clasps her pockets, and it drops out onto the beige bathroom rug. There's no name assigned to the number, but that's when she remembers Javis, causing her to erupt in an uncontrollable cry. She picks it up and listens.

"Hello? Alexis?"

A deep wail leaves her body as she cradles the phone. "Javis," she cries. "Javis...I messed up. I messed up really bad."

"It's over now, Alexis. Whatever you did in the past, it's over now," he responds to her tears as he sits on his bed, thinking mostly of his mother who needs immediate care, having no idea that Alexis just killed someone else.

At the sound of his words, Alexis realizes that despite what she just revealed, he still doesn't know all of her truth about the past and present, so she wipes her eyes and swallows her confession, although the sight of Zeena's thrusting about as she died on the floor of her house won't disappear. She takes another deep breath, wipes the tears from her face, and gets undressed. "Yeah, you're right. I'm just glad you forgive me," she continues as she reaches into her medicine cabinet to pull out a razor. Then, just as Javis continues to encourage her, she slices a small portion of the inside of her thigh to take the emotional pain away. His words take care of the rest.

DECEPTION

AT

GABRIEL'S

TRAILS

II

DECEPTION AT GABRIEL'S TRAILS II

The true nature of the street life is a beast, being run by smoke and mirrors, and a young lady finds out just how foggy her life can get when she is confronted in a deadly game that she decided to play with the most cut-throat killer in Gabriel's Trails. The only question is who will outwit the other and win in the end?

Out of breath and out of time, Tony leaps toward the hallway and runs toward the back sliding door, dropping his cellular phone as he makes the turn at the couch. "Shit!" The whole thing comes apart, the battery sliding one place and the phone another. Scurrying across the floor he locates the front of the phone and minutes later the back, however, the house is pitch black inside, making it difficult to find the one piece he needs to make the phone work – the battery.

"Dammit, fuck!" He reaches underneath the couch and cautiously turns on his flashlight, careful to hide the light from the windows, as he shines it underneath. He moves the light from side to side but sees nothing. "Come on, come on," he growls, switching the light off and feeling across the floor when there's movement at the front door. Like he sees a ghost, he turns to face the door and all his bodily functions seem to shut down for seconds as he listens to keys rattle. Before the door opens, he bolts toward the sliding door, leaving his battery behind as he pulls the door shut and hurdles across the grass.

His feet don't move fast enough as his destination appears too far away. Before going into the house, he parked his car two blocks away in order to make people believe he is one place when really he is in another. As he hustles as fast as he can in the darkness of night, he looks down at his phone realizing that he only has seconds before anyone notices he was there. His thoughts are on his battery as he comes closer to his way out of sight. Quickly, he shoots a glance back at the house, and the lights are already on by the time he turns the corner, moving adjacent to an abandoned home in order to catch his breath.

Coughing violently, he leans over, resting his hands onto his knees before sitting on the ground in pain from struggling to breathe. He reaches inside his pocket, pulls out his inhaler, shakes it up, and inhales the medication that will open up his lungs so that he can get more oxygen.

"I can't believe this shit," he heaves, completely out of breath and taking a second puff of his inhaler. "There wasn't shit inside that fuckin' place. Almost got my ass killed for nothing." He peeps back around the condo in order to see if anyone has come out to follow him, and he sees that all is clear. Removing his backpack, he shoves the parts of his phone inside and pulls out a shirt that he yanks down over his head, all of this to mask what he is wearing underneath in case someone saw him running. It's not more than two minutes before he's off again, this time walking calmly down the streets of Gabriel's Trails toward his car as if he's done nothing wrong on the crowded streets that never seem to sleep.

"Chief," Tryina calls, putting her hands out, stopping him at the door. However, he doesn't stop moving forward until she stalls him with another push. "Chief, stop," she commands silently as she watches the blinds of the sliding door move with the wind through a small opening. Then, she turns to face Chief with fear in her eyes. "Someone's in here."

Without hesitation, he pulls Tryina back outside while ordering two others who are at his car to make their rounds, or in other words, find the culprit. The men split up in opposite directions, already searching for an odd man out of the people they run into on the sidewalks. Meanwhile, Chief pulls out his pistol. Then, he hands Tryina his other pistol, and she has no choice but to take it. She knows this world, and she's not ignorant to the fact that she can either help them or be on her own. She's not willing to be on her own.

That would mean she has a target on her head at all times with no help for the fight.

"Stay at the door…pistol down, face up, trigger ready."

Tryina nods although she is slightly shaken but as ready as she can be because she has no choice. Someone may be after her or even after her money. She stands watch as Chief combs through the house like he's done it before, and after finding no one, she watches him walk toward the sliding door and then outside. Tryina remains frozen in her stance as her pulse continues to rise while she holds the pistol in place, prepared to shoot at any unknown face.

Chief stands tall and uneffected by the brazenness of anyone to step foot on land that has always and will forever be known as that which belongs to the fallen hustlers of Gabriel's Trails. Tryina's home is considered off limits to any and everyone minus those who keep watch over her day and night out of loyalty, respect, and most of all the money that is willed by blood and nothing else to Tryina until it all runs out. It's Chief who is the last man standing and presiding over all of Gabriel's Trails now, and although he is rarely seen making a noise of anything at anytime, most know when he is seen, someone will die.

He looks to the left and right, but no one is seen running away. As he starts to move forward, a neighbor exits his back door and stares directly into Chief's eyes. Then, this same man he points to his right while stating the perpetrators name out loud.

Chief gets on his cell phone because he knows exactly who it is, even without a last name. He knows it's no other than Tryina's friend, Macy's man, and he goes after him. Seconds later, someone picks up on the other end of the phone, and Chief speaks, "It's Tony. Get him. Bring him back here alive. Walk with him, and don't draw the wrong attention. If he won't walk back, kill him. Leave him right there on the street, so people know. That's the only attention we need."

Tony's legs dangle from his car as he lounges back on the trunk in an attempt to cover up his guilt. A couple of people walk by who are familiar with him and chat, however, they keep walking by, leaving him an easy target in the dark of night by the two men who approach. Tony doesn't see them initially, however, as he looks further down the road at two men walking at about the same speed toward his car, he shuffles slightly to remove the book bag from his back. Then, he flashes a smile to onlookers who also see who is coming down the road, guns already visible.

From there, Tony eases off of the trunk, takes his bag into the palm of his hand, and calmly moves toward the driver's side door before jumping inside. Without warning, gunshots ring out, and people drop to the ground as he finds the keys to start the car, but as he's starting it, he another barrage of gunshots land against his car from every way.

"Alright! Alright!" he yells covering his head in terror as the shots land against the car. His vehicle drops onto the street, alerting him to the fact that he has no more wheels, and he becomes brutally aware as they're shooting that they aren't shooting to kill. With death breathing down his back, he glances out of the window only to see them waiting as there is a cease fire. Weeping and nearly completely soaked in his pants, the small time drug dealer gets out of the car, dropping to the ground on both his knees with his head down and hands up. He doesn't say a word and is too ashamed to look up and face the people who are watching although pretending to hide.

Several men come out of the dark with pistols ready, adding a sense of dread to any neighbors who could potentially call law enforcement. The horror about Gabriel's Trails is that no one knows everyone who's on the payroll, so to snitch is a dangerous thing. This is how any secret that goes on in the Trails stays there and is handled internally.

"Get up, Tony," one of the men address him with a pistol against his lowered head. "Walk with us to Tryina's place."

"That's not my girl, man," Tony stresses, trying to divert their justification for approaching him in such a deadly way.

"Are you coming?"

The question is rhetorical, and Tony knows it, therefore, he refrains from answering because a negative response could positively land him in a grave. Without parting his lips to say another word, Tony gets up from the ground as the man with the pistol at his head even helps him up.

"Did you piss yourself, man?" he laughs like everything is funny about how the night is going. "You smell like shit?"

Instead of answering, Tony continues to stand as tall as he can, despite his urine soaked pants and distraught nerves. There is an unspoken code in the streets of Gabriel's Trails for gangsters, whether small time like Tony, or the top of the line, and that is to go to death like a man if it's a must. It makes those living feel better about how a man leaves, and it makes the dead realize who they're getting. Both see the same thing...strength and fearlessness.

As Tony walks all on his own with two men ready to shoot him in the back if he even motions wrong, he's already formulating a story about where he was during the robbery that places him nowhere near the scene. Just as if he would do if he had to sit in front of cops, his plans are to keep silent for as long as he can until someone pulls his card. It is only then he will talk because unlike with cops, his only lawyer will be his word. Therefore, he has to make his story good and convincing.

It's not ten minutes before they make it back to Tryina's place, and as he walks inside the sliding door that he previously exited, he comes face to face with a gun toting Tryina. She stands there in her cut up jeans, barefoot and braids pulled up into a knot on the side of her head. He then begins his spill.

"Tryina, man…what's this, girl? You sent these people for me?"

"No. Who sent you?" she responds, angered to no end with thoughts racing through her mind about why he was in her house. She has her own ideas, but fail to trust those hunches because it could be devastating.

"Who sent me? What the hell you mean who sent me? Sent me where? Hell, sent me when? These fools came up to me at my car...that's fucked the hell up now, by the damn way, with bullet holes and shit…and I don't know what the fuck for." He looks around and then asks, "Well, at least let me sit down and shit, T, damn. Treatin' me like you don't know me. Can you get that damn gun out of my face, homey?" Tony is very young and sounds very dumb to those around him who have many more years and ears dealing in the streets. They can smell what the novice Tony has yet to be able to sense, and the one thing they sense is that his story is full of fabrication.

"Sit down, Tony," a voice says from the hallway, and when the person who spoke appears in the living room, he's tossing something into the air. "Where the fuck is your phone?"

"I don't have my phone. It's back at the car. They shot at me and shit, so I'm not fuckin' worried about a damn phone. Hell, I'll buy you one if you want one that bad, damn!" Tony already knows what they've found, but there's no way he is confessing to anything.

"Stand him up."

"All this for my phone, Chief? Hold up, hold up, I can stand up myself," he retorts, firmly moving away from the two men holding pistols at his back to force him into rising from the loveseat faster. "Shit, Chief, you just told me to sit down, man!" He glances at Tryina who stands there with blood shot eyes in disbelief over what is transpiring with Tony being her best friend's boyfriend, and although he's never set foot in her house, it's probably safe for her to assume Macy let some of her secrets leak. Just the thought of this scenario gives her a sore pain in her heart, and the only way she can hide it is through pushing through a rage to which she's never fully released. She's always on the losing end, and this time, she plans on making things different. Maybe she is too nice.

"Tryina? Tell them I've never even been in here. I wouldn't have a reason to be here in the first place."

"What's your phone number, Tony?"

Tony flashes a terrified glance at Chief who stands closer to him now, so close that Tony can trace the tapered cut on his beard that matches the low cut fade perfectly that lines his head. There's no sweat falling from his dark skin just as the rumor has it about the man everyone knows as

Chief. Even when it's as hot as it is outside, his face is cold as ice, dry as the desert. This is Tony's first time standing this close to Chief, and as tough as he desires to be, he is shaken by what he sees…a man with a will to kill in his eyes.

"Man, I…I can't remember my own phone number off the top…" he stutters.

"You see this?" he asks, raising a cell phone battery. "Tryina has her phone, don't you, sis?" he calls her out of loyalty toward her deceased brother. She nods while Tony's eyes fixate onto his lost cell phone battery like a magnet. His knees weaken almost immediately, so he shuffles his feet, cracks a grin and says, "Yeah, it's a battery."

"Your motha' fuckin' phone better ring, and that shit better ring right now. What's the number?"

"But, Chief…"

"Did you have an accident while you were walking around in here tonight? Dropping shit on the floor?"

"How is a battery gonna say anything about me, huh?"

"You deal because I let you deal," he states, referring to Tony's small time drug hustle. "Your phone is always on…just like mine," he responds as the others pat him down to find no phone. When they come up empty, Chief makes another call to other hit men in the area near Tony's car. Tony reacts in anger.

"Man, my car is out there all shot up and shit, and you're gonna have people go in my shit? Fuck that, let me go." Jumping toward the back door, Tony is knocked back to his knees, but he refuses to stop fighting because he knows that Chief is about to find all the evidence he needs to execute him. It isn't five minutes after Chief makes his phone call that his cell phone rings back. Chief answers, and without a word, ends the call only to place a gun directly at Tony's forehead. Before the trigger is pulled, Tryina begins to dial.

"Wait a minute, Chief."

**

Her hair is soaked as she steps out of the shower. The blood that drains from the wound she gave herself on her inner thigh has slowed while she is now able to concentrate on facing the world once again after what she has done. After hanging up the phone with Javis, he's agreed to meet her in an hour at the same spot they departed from one another. In the meantime, she must conceal what she's done from the two people who may be able to interpret her movements and emotions the best in the world – her mother and father.

She opens the bathroom door after drying off and goes to slide on her robe. Everything is still moving in slow motion since she killed Zeena, and as she walks out of her room, her mom is already coming toward her.

"I didn't even hear you come inside. You've taken a shower and everything. Come on downstairs. Oh, and how was the party?"

Stunned enough to stop in her tracks as the words come forth from her mom's mouth, she doesn't know how to answer. Therefore, she shoves a smile onto her face and looks toward the floor, diverting attention from the question.

She had no idea her mother knew where she was earlier. "Ouch, my foot."

"What's wrong, Alexis?"

"I think I hurt my foot. It'll be okay. I'll be downstairs in a minute."

"Great because we were both waiting on you. After you said you wanted to launch your own magazine, we decided to connect you with some of the people I know who you could possibly intern with on the road to founding yours." She reaches in and gives her a kiss on the cheek along with a big squeeze as if she was still thirteen years old and wet behind the ears. "Oh and when you get down, you can tell us all about the party."

"It's late, ma."

As her mother walks away, she pauses and appears puzzled as she turns back to face Alexis. "Since when is eleven o'clock late for you...or us for that matter? Business never sleeps. Remember that," she sings as she heads off, excited that her only child wants to become a writer and founder of her own magazine.

Alexis watches as her mother goes downstairs, and instead of lagging behind like she wants to do, she heads down after her. The sooner she can get the meeting over the better. To Alexis, there is really no sense in stalling. Speaking with her parents is inevitable as she has yet to move out.

They all meet in the entertainment room which has been decorated the same exact way from six years ago. It's a room she rarely likes to enter anymore because she remains haunted by the memory of the first person she killed. She remembers how he held her and caressed her body right in this same room. She loved him so much, and really believed they would one day be together, away from everyone who spoke otherwise. Alexis stares at him in the mirrors that line the walls of the room and watches him with her until...

"Alexis. Stop staring and come on over here. Sit down," her mother calls. "Good Lord, you act like you've seen a ghost or something every time you come over here." Her mother doesn't know just how accurate her statement is as Alexis takes her eyes off of the mirror and pays attention to her mother. Her dad is also there who she stubbornly ignores as he turns on the flat screen that is perched high on the sound proof wall. Alexis takes a seat as she already knows nothing will be discussed until after the first half of the news ends. Before she even leans back into the chair next to her mother, tension grows from the deepest part of her soul at the report that flashes across the screen.

"This just in, there has been a murder at the home of Congressman Castles tonight, and the victim is his own daughter, his only daughter, Ms. Zeena Castles. The reports are sketchy at the moment because word is just now coming in to the station, however, it can be confirmed that the body is in fact the body of his daughter. The police, as of yet, have no suspect, but she is reported to have been found not breathing and possibly attacked directly inside the home by a perpetrator, but we will keep you updated when more details are available. If there is anyone in the area who may know anything, investigators ask for immediate help by calling the number at the bottom of the screen."

"Oh my God! Michael!" Alexis' mom grabs her daughter's hand and squeezes while she starts to weep and feel all over Alexis' face as if she's the one that died. Alexis blankly watches her mom's concern as she checks her over to make certain she is fine while thanking God she is alive. As Lorah notices the lack of emotion on her daughter's face, she places her hand onto Alexis' chest and notices that her heart is beating furiously. "Oh dear Lord, Michael, she's in shock. Bring me some water or something. Don't just sit there. You're a doctor. Her friend just died, dammit. She's breaking down in here, and she was just there! She was just there, dammit, Michael!"

This is furthest from the truth. As Lorah brings her daughter in closer to her, she rests her head on her mother's shoulder. She now faces her father who has finally turned his attention from the television to find the truth in his daughter's eyes. A lone tear falls from Alexis' face, and as it does, her robe falls open to reveal blood trickling from a cut on her thigh. His eyes drop down at the revelation, just one other thing he's helped hide from his wife about his own daughter. With all his power, he slams the remote control atop the marble table, breaking it to pieces as Lorah jumps away from her grieving daughter and yells while he storms from the room.

"Michael! Just what the hell is wrong with you?"

Alexis only sits there, realizing that her own father is on his way to fix everything as he always does because as she was raised to believe – money conquers all. As she watches her mother move to clean up the broken remote, she comes to grips with the fact that she doesn't believe that lie anymore. She then pulls her robe back together again as she stares at the television, awaiting the next news report on the murder to which only she can fill in the minute details. She still feels no remorse. She did what she had to do to a female who'd already snitched her out.

**

"Well, fuck me!" Macy screams as she shakes her small television. "How the fuck did she die?" Both her hands hold her head like she's keeping it from exploding as she turns around in circles not comprehending what is going on. "Shit!" Her nice, preppy hairdo and outfit look like a sure fit for identification, so she runs to her room and undresses. "Somebody saw me. Dammit, everybody saw me! These mother fuckers never sleep in this place." Breathing heavily, she takes off all her clothes and loosens her hair from the neat bun she showed off earlier. Pulling clothing out of her drawers, she tosses on some jeans, a baseball cap and an orange shirt. Before she does anything else, she runs back into the living room and stares at Zeena's cell phone.

It sits there on her couch, and Macy doesn't know what to do with it except stare at it like it's the plague. "Fuck!" she panics while pacing back and forth before remembering that the phone could be traced back to her place. Making a dash to turn it off, there's a ring which causes her to jump back away from the phone in horror. However, it isn't Zeena's phone that rings, but her own.

"Hello, hello," she answers without finding out who it is on the other end. It's Tryina. She quickly stares back at the television, and then places her undivided attention on the conversation. Her pulse races but she slows her breathing down purposely as she glances up at her windows and front door to make certain they are secure.

"Macy," says the person on the other end of the line.

Scurrying to her long black curtains, she peeps out of the window, and when she sees no one there, she answers while placing her attention back on the dead girl's phone. "Hi, Tryina," she pauses, "Look, I made it back home, and I was gonna call you to say I'm sorry for leaving you back there and acting like I did. I suppose you're still walking home and all…I'm sorry, girl." she continues with excuses while listening out for any sign that she needs to escape Gabriel's Trails while she still has time. "You wanna come over and get something else to eat. I'm warming up some food. You know, that pizza wasn't…"

"No, I'm good. I accept your apology though."

"Thank you, T. You know how I get when I'm trying to impress somebody," she rambles nervously, still not able to pinpoint if something has been discovered on Tryina's end.

"Yeah. You go overboard. You always go overboard, don't you, Macy?" She waits on Macy to answer through the anxiety she has already detected in her voice, but when Macy remains silent, she continues, realizing that her best friend may have betrayed her in the worst way. "You know what, Macy," she continues in a perkier voice, "I know you've heard some stuff, and I never got into detail with you about anything because I can't. Just know that I didn't walk home like you think. I took a ride home with someone I needed to take a ride home with, and it was that girl named Alexis who brought the pizza. I nearly beat her ass. That shit felt good, too. I didn't even realize…"

Macy's face falls to the floor, and she looks like she's seen a ghost. The name she'd heard numerous times a long time ago just re-emerged in her memory. There was chatter all around Gabriel's Trails about a girl with a similar sounding name – Alexis - that she'd heard about, but it was before her and Tryina had gotten as close as they are now. She'd heard bits and pieces of a story, about how a rich girl destroyed the legend of the family of Bain, but she'd always shut her ears to it back then. It was just too dangerous to discuss, and she, just like everyone else, stayed out of the affairs of the gangster known as Bain. Back then, even community conversations were controlled out of pure fear. The terror is more dismantled more now than it ever was although still dangerous, but to Macy's shock, the terror isn't as dismantled as she thought, proving her comfort level with Tryina, who never shows a violent side, is all a mirage. Whatever her brother had in him, it's finally risen up in her as well. Macy now realizes that she's mistaken Tryina for a soft target and should have never pretended to be her friend versus associate.

"What do you mean, you nearly beat her ass, T?" she asks, growing increasingly paranoid, while searching her phone for a text message or some sign that her boyfriend got out of Tryina's house undetected. She finds none.

"Just what I said. I wasn't about all that gangster stuff, but this...this is for my brother...and the man who saved my life when I was a child. Gabriel's Trails is going to remember both their names and how to never cross anyone in my family again. Haven't you ever gotten tired of trying to live right and everything just goes wrong all the time?"

A jolt of fear shoots through Macy's body before she responds in agreeance although fully aware that the whole tone of the conversation may be a threat to her. "Well, if you say she asked for it, then she asked for it. And I know you can't bring me in on everything that you and your family has to do. I can't say I want to be in on it either, T, but I thought you never wanted to be like your brother and the rest of them? I mean, you always talked trash..." Her eyes travel toward her front door and comb over it once again, becoming overwhelmed with the dread that could soon possibly stand on the other side.

"That little rich girl took everything from me back then, came and *robbed me* of everything I had...indirectly but still…she's the root." Tryina pauses before speaking again as she stops the tears from exiting her eyes. "The worst part about it is she gets to walk free and I don't. Back then, I didn't understand, Macy. But you have to stand in my shoes, and only then will you know how it feels to stand face to face with the reason for your life's dreams being torn apart. This isn't something I want to do. It's what I have to do. I've always said that if I saw her, I would hurt her, if I couldn't help myself. The shit suffocates me at night, Macy," she continues in a low, flat tone, having been silently tormented every day since death occurred all around her. "She's the only enemy I know, and with an enemy like that, like my brother used to always say, you take 'em out before they do it to you." There's a long pause which worsens Macy's anxiety.

Nothing but complete silence overwhelms Macy. She is frozen in despair at a person she thought would never hurt a fly, but for the first time in Macy's life, she understands how to separate desire from need. Need is much more powerful.

"Anyway, the fight happened at the entrance of the neighborhood, Macy, and I'm just now walking up to my place. You wanna meet me there? I need some company. I'm pissed, and I need some leverage for my mental state before I do something I'll regret."

"Sure, yeah, yeah…I'll come," responds Macy, feeling a bit relieved that Tryina says she hasn't made it back to the house. "Give me a few minutes and I'll meet you there. Anything for my sister, right?"

"For life."

Macy listens as the phone call ends. Quickly, she concocts a way to distance herself from her own boyfriend just in case she's being set up. She grabs a pen and finds her journal. She hasn't written inside it in days, so she decides to date this newest entry in the past, as far back as she can go. Then she begins to write…"*I hate his ass. I can't believe he hit me in my face and threatened to kill me because I wouldn't tell him shit about Tryina and her money. I love that girl. Fuck him. Talking about I'm his and his forever. Fuck him. If I had the nerve, I'd shoot his ass myself before he kills me for trying to leave.*"

After writing that one, she rushes over to her drawer and finds another pen, this time one with blue ink. She sits back down and writes again, this time dated with yesterday's date. She writes, *"I broke up with his ass. He said he was gonna go through with something stupid, but I bet he won't. He doesn't have the balls for it. Especially when he gets found out, he's dead. I can't be involved with a stupid dude that might get me killed along with his dumb ass. Fuck that. If he goes through with anything, my ass is gonna snitch. Pay back. No man hits me."*

She glances at the clock on the wall. Because her boyfriend hasn't called her back, a drowning sensation overtakes her, and the weight of just her chest alone feels too heavy for her to carry. She drifts to her bed which is covered with a faux satin comforter that she purchased a year ago when she'd set her sights on gaining more money and never living the poor life she has in Gabriel's Trails any longer.

She's a runaway, and it is Gabriel's Trails that seemed to fit her life back then, believing it was cool to live with others until she stole and swindled enough money inconspicuously to live on her own. When she finally became able to rent her own place in the neighborhood, she did, but as she looks around at the four walls of her bedroom, it may be time to move on once again and start over. Macy knows she's taken things too far and with the wrong people, and this time, her thieving ways may have caused her to cross paths with the wrong pile of cash. Either way it goes, she won't make it out of Gabriel's Trails alive if anyone has linked her to what her and her boyfriend have concocted. Therefore, she knows she has to play the game on out, meet Tryina at her home, and go from there with the deck stacked against her man and in her favor...just in case.

There's money she keeps underneath her mattress and also some in the floor of her closet. After retrieving it all, she sits back on her bed growing impatient as she waits on a call from her boyfriend before leaving. Five minutes go by, and nothing. She doesn't call him because she has no idea if it's safe to do so, therefore, she sets off with cash and a bag of clothes that she puts in the trunk of her car, and the one thing she needs to remove from her residence - Zeena's cell phone.

**

"Congressman? Congressman Castles," he calls to a tall, lanky dark-skinned gentleman wearing slacks and a polo shirt who is pulling into the driveway of his home. The police presence is overbearing inside the Dominion Lakes neighborhood as officers are already going house to house in the middle of the night to find out if anyone saw anything pertaining to the murder of Zeena Castles, the congressman's daughter.

"Oh dear God, Jordan. Jordan!" a petite African American woman with blood on her hands screams as she falls to the ground, unable to be consoled. The congressman runs toward her, ignoring everyone else who calls his name. When he reaches her, he only falls to the ground and holds her in his arms while everyone watches in dismay.

"I know, sweetheart, I know. I have to go in there. I have to see my daughter," he chokes back tears as he lifts her from the ground along with himself.

"They won't let me back inside, Jordan. That's my baby in there," she hollers hysterically. "That's my only baby!"

"Like hell they won't." He shoves off of her and muscles his way toward his front door where investigators are combing the scene.

"Congressman Castles, please, sir, if you would step aside."

"Step aside? That's my daughter in there, and this is my house. You step aside!" he points into his home and then reaches up to move the officer. The officer continues to stand in front of him, understanding why he feels the need to go inside, however, it's crucial the investigation isn't hindered by his presence. "Didn't you hear me? I said move!" Finally he strikes toward the officer's shoulder, and two other officers quickly come to subdue him. Unfortunately, as he is taken down, he catches a glimpse of his daughter as she lies there on the foyer floor dead.

All of the congressman's strength leaves him, and he ends up just like his wife, on the ground with no hope left. Alexis' father is the first one over to help pry him away from the police officers.

"Congressman Castles, I'm right here, I'm right here by your side," he speaks as the congressman recognizes the voice and stares directly into the Caucasian man he knows as the surgeon that lives down the street.

"Dr. Balentine…they killed my daughter in there. Can you go and help her? Please…she might come back. Can you double check?"

"Congressman," he responds, shifting his eyes to see inside the home through the ajar front door. "I'll try. Just wait here. I'll tell you what I can tell you, but just remain here." Not feeling comfortable about rejecting the congressman without giving some effort to his request, he has a discussion with one of the investigators who then looks over at Congressman Castles who gives him a nod. After they finish speaking, Dr. Balentine walks back to Congressman Castles, escorts him to the side of the house, and begins again.

"First I want to invite both you and your wife to my home tonight, and for as long as you like. We have plenty room to spare, but I have to tell you…things aren't good, Congressman. She hasn't taken a breath in over an hour. She's gone." Alexis' father observes Congressman Castles' eyes and it's as if he's hearing the grievous words about his daughter for the first time. That's when he finally falls to the ground and wails, transforming from a man who appeared to have more control over himself when he pulled up in the yard to a man who is having a difficult time even taking another breath of life.

"Michael, that's my child. That's my only baby. Who would kill my daughter?" he yells, pounding his chest like he could murder the person who did it with his bare hands.

"Come on, you and your wife. I'll alert the cops to where you will be…with me. That way, you can avoid the media circus that is bound to come around, even more than they are now. Here, come on…" he states, lifting his neighbor from the ground. "You're gonna get through this, and they will catch who did this really soon. Trust me. They will be caught."

They both walk over to his distraught wife, Mr. Balentine takes the car keys from the congressman, and drives them to his home. When he walks inside, Alexis is sitting on the staircase wiping her eyes from fatigue although it mimics sadness. However when she watches the next two people come through the front door, her wiping ceases to meet the cold stare of her father.

"Alexis," he calls, "Go upstairs. Get some rest."

**

The car stops just short of the curb, and she stares forward. Her heart beats faster than it's ever beat before, and when she turns to face Tryina's home, there isn't anyone lurking around in the darkness suspiciously. When she looks to the left, the regular amount of people who usually hang out at night in front of their condos are doing just that, having a good time. No one seems to be afraid. While she's looking around, she doesn't see any sign of her boyfriend, therefore, she steps out of the car, careful not to disclose any signs of discomfort because she feels like she's being watched.

"Stop being so paranoid," she whispers to herself as she leans down purposely to wipe her pants. "You got this," she continues, raising herself back up, waving to someone across the street while flashing her usual big smile, skips onto the sidewalk before cutting through the grass to Tryina's front door. She can barely swallow her own spit because her throat trembles and feels extremely tight due to her collapsed nerves. "Feel like I'm having a damn stroke. Chill, self, just chill." Her self-motivating stops as she knocks on the door and yells, "Tryina, it's me. Open up."

No one comes to the door, and this allows Macy to breathe a sigh of relief. She also hears nothing inside from where she stands, so it seems all is calm. Therefore, she knocks again, and this time, right after she knocks, she turns her back to the door. Finally she hears the locks moving along with the door knob, and when she turns back to face the door, it's Tryina. Macy freezes, and the smile she started with fades quickly. She realizes she has everything to worry about when Tryina steps to the side and directly in front of her, standing in the living room, is Chief with the barrel of a gun pointed directly at her.

"Come in, Macy."

Her knees become frail and feel like they can collapse at any second. She can't run. She's not that stupid. Tryina answering the door is all for appearance's sake for the people across the street. It's so dark in the house that no one can see inside, and at the same time, Macy can feel the danger lurking behind her. Instead of turning to face the dangers that she knows Chief has at her back, she stares intently back into Tryina's eyes as if she doesn't know what's going on.

"Are you serious? Why is Chief pointing a gun at me?" Then, she glances down near Tryina's thigh and notices the glock. "You, too?"

"Come inside, Macy."

Macy can clearly see the tears welling up inside Tryina's eyes, but she can't tell if it's sadness or rage. Without any choice, she steps fearfully inside the condo, hoping that she can talk her way out of what she believes has been a snitch job – her boyfriend implicating her instead of him taking the fall all alone. Chief's gun doesn't falter as she walks steadily and directly into it, purposely promoting her confusion like a banner as her hands stretch out to her sides. The door slams behind her causing fear to rip through to her core as she believes it's a gun shot from the pistol that's aimed directly in between her eyes.

"Stop right there, Macy," Tryina orders from behind her and then asks, "Why did you do it?"

Macy turns her head to the side to speak to Tryina but keeps her body facing Chief, confident that she's able to persuade her friend into believing something other than what is really going on. "Do what, T? I didn't mean to get so damn angry at you at the party, but do you really think I need to die behind it?"

"This isn't about some mother fuckin' party, and your ass knows it. Walk," commands Chief. Macy then walks forward, and just as she steps into the living room area, she sees her boyfriend being held down by the force of another gun pointing directly at the back of his head while he sits on a chair. "Sit your ass down in that chair beside your man. That is your man, right?"

Macy quickly faces a teary eyed but enraged Tryina, and then looks back down at her boyfriend who sits there like he has nothing left to face but death. She then speaks, "What's going on?"

"Is this your man?"

"He used to be."

"Bitch, fuck you!" Tony lashes out.

"No, I'm not! No I'm not lying!" she screams as she drops to the floor, afraid that Chief will kill her. "I don't know what he's done but we broke up days ago. Tryina," she calls, "You have to believe me on this. He said he was gonna kill me. He wouldn't let me go, I swear."

"You never told me you two broke up," Tryina interjects her pleas as she points the gun at the chest of the female she considered a sister just hours ago.

"Chief!" She turns frantically toward him and then back at Tryina while her boyfriend continuously drowns her out with his words, shouting that she was in on the whole robbery. "He's lying! Wait…" she begs as she holds her hands out in the air in surrender. "I can prove it. I can…I can prove it. My proof is at the house. I swear. Tryina, you can see for yourself. All of you can see with your own eyes."

"She's lyin'!" Tony reacts, throwing his fists in a rage. "Fuck her. It was her damn idea! Greedy ass. That's my damn girl, and if I gotta damn die because of her back stabbin' ass, then shoot her ugly ass, too. Shit. Give a fuck." He pauses then leans back into the chair, tapping the pistol with the back of his head. "Hell, kill her ass first so I can see it. That's all my ass asks. I did this shit for her."

"Chief, he's lying. I love Tryina. You know Tony's corrupt. You know it. He swore he would kill me, and I tried to break it off with him, but he told me he would kill me if I walked around these streets like a single woman. Tryina…you haven't even seen me with him in days, have you?" Tryina doesn't answer, so Macy continues, "Chief, come with me to my place. I'll prove it to you. It's all in my journal."

"Sit down in the chair next to your man Tony right there, and Tony don't you touch her ass either. Tryina," he says while turning to face her, "Round 'em up. Tell 'em we're going for a ride. Don't wanna fuckin' kill your friend behind this small timer right here if I don't have to," he smiles while noticing her grief. "Cheer up, lil sis. I'm your brother's keeper, even while he's in the grave." Before he turns back around and as Tryina walks away from the scene, Macy knocks something into the cushion of the loveseat and readjusts herself to get as close to the armrest as she can, pretending that it's all because of her not wanting to be next to Tony.

"When we walk out of here, our guns will be out of sight. Homey that's in the car out there with those tinted windows will be aiming to kill your ass if you run. I don't fuckin' chase anyone," he says to Macy. "When I say get up, you get up, walk to the car, and we go. I'll be behind you."

"I got it." Macy knows that her nervousness is mistaken for fear, thus, realizing it's the best time to do nothing but think. Various scenarios run through her head as she ponders what she will do and say once she gets back to her place. On top of that, she's leaving Zeena's cell phone in Tryina's loveseat. If it rings too soon or at all, the last place she wants to do is be around when it happens. Her only option now is to flee as soon as Chief clears her of any wrong doing, and that's her only concern as she glances at Tony who is completely irate. She can care less about his life if it means saving hers. Ten minutes go by, and it's within that time that Macy is back at her home with Chief walking in behind her.

The front door closes, but she doesn't move a muscle until Chief gives her permission. When he does, Macy rushes to where she placed her journal, between the waste basket and the television stand on a magazine rack. Then, she sits down on the couch as she watches Chief with the pistol, aiming it right at her body. "See...see...I write everything down in here. You can see for yourself." She lays it out on the sofa, flipping through the pages as if she doesn't know where she wrote the fabricated lines.

Chief laughs at her gesture of asking him to come over and read anything. "Bring your ass over here and hold that book up so I can read it, both your hands on the book, and if you move one of your hands from that book, I'll kill your ass right here on your mother fuckin' floor. Nobody will hear shit because I'll kill their asses, too."

Feeling like she's going to pass out, her mouth dries, and because her throat can no longer take the nervousness, and she vomits on the floor. Chief doesn't make one move to help her as he's seen people regurgitate out of fear many times before, coming out one end or another when people stare death in the face. He waits on her to finish, and when she finally gets her wind back, she walks over to him, book in hand, and holds it up to his face, quivering in despair.

Her fingers are glued to the pages as she stares at the cover of the journal while he reads. She doesn't see the gun nor the look on his face as he reads, and the fact that she doesn't know if he will pull the trigger on her creates a maddening sensation, like the walls are closing in.

"There's another page," she stutters. "It says where I broke up with him. May I turn the page, please?"

"Turn that shit because what you showed me is that you knew about a plan and didn't say shit about it."

Macy turns the page to the other fabricated concoction, and as he reads, Chief leans to the side and looks at her face. "Move that book down a little bit." He begins to scan her body. "Where the hell did he hit you?"

"In my stomach. He punched me in my stomach," she lies, realizing that Chief is searching for visible evidence of her life being threatened by Tony. "Said he doesn't want to walk around and claim a female who has a messed up face, so that's why…he hit me in my stomach."

Chief takes a deep breath, believes Macy to a point, but solidifies her story with an option of revenge. "You wanna go back over there and kill him?"

"I haven't ever killed anyone before. I don't hate him, but I…"

"This man was about to rob your friend, and he punched you in the stomach. You got a clean getaway. Kill him." Chief says as he toys with her mind. "He's gonna die anyway, right? Get your revenge before he hits that fuckin' dust."

Tears flow down her face, but she doesn't want to reject any offer he throws out. She imagines herself killing someone, and out of all the crimes she's ever committed, murder would end up being the ultimate one, something she feels she could never survive. Chief's face blurs through her tears, but although her mind wants to say no, her mouth utters a silent, "I'll do it."

A satisfied Chief pulls back his pistol and snatches the journal from her hand, tossing it to the floor. "Well, let's ride. Ladies first."

Macy stands there frozen at first, in disbelief that she actually made it out alive with her excuses. She walks beyond Chief to her front door of freedom but stops in her tracks when she hears his phone ring.

"Don't move, Macy. Stay right there until I give you the word." He looks at his phone puzzled and answers. As he speaks, his entire demeanor changes into anger. He stares at the back of Macy's head, but doesn't say a word. Instead, he aims aims at the back of her head. "Turn around, baby."

Confused, she stares at the door knob, pretending not to hear what he just said. Standing only three feet away from it, if she lifts her hand and leans, she can run, but he speaks again. This time, she feels the pistol press against her skull as she throws her hands up, grits her teeth and listens to his voice.

"You lied to me."

"What?"

He leans in to her right ear and answers her question in a dull whisper, "His cell phone." He pulls the trigger at the back of her head, and Macy falls to her knees reaching for the door knob as Chief walks to the door, opens it, and lets himself out, shutting it slowly as he watches her eyes close and her body collapse onto the floor, right next to the journal.

Tryina falls against the wall as she hears the gun go off through the phone of Chief's running partner. The firm grip she has on the pistol loosens, but before it drops, he snatches it from her while she becomes deafened by the sound of Tony yelling at the top of his lungs at the gunshot he heard as well.

"Hold this shit like Chief told you to do."

Tryina feels nothing. Her emotions are as blank as the expression on her face. Looking down at the pistol once again, she pulls it from his hand, and then turns to face Tony. Her grip around the trigger is tighter than before, and her senses are now completely aware of the betrayal that is all around her.

"Tryina! You ain't no killer. You don't know the whole story. Just wait on Chief to get back," he pleads. "I can explain that," he continues as Tryina stares down at his cell phone, now all put together with the missing battery, which ended up being the link between Macy's involvement in the botched robbery. There were text messages, even a recent phone call not too long ago, that explains everything they have been trying to deny.

Tryina aims the gun. There is a sound at the front door. She already knows who it is, so she pulls the trigger. She doesn't need permission. She'll never allow anyone to betray her again. The bullet catches Tony in the chest, he falls backwards onto the loveseat, and before he even bleeds out, the fellas lift him up in the air as Chief watches at the doorway.

"Bury him in the trails. When they find Macy, they'll find their main suspect for this case laying right there beside her on that damn floor in a fuckin' book. He's already long gone, and they'll never find him," he says referring to a dead Tony. Chief then addresses Tryina. "Go on about your life…normally. Keep that pistol even though nobody else is coming."

All the men exit through the back as a car pulls up with the back door already open. It all happens in less than five minutes, and as Tony's dead body is driven off to be buried in one of the trails, Tryina stands there eyeballing the loveseat. She's watching his body die continuously, and yet she still feels nothing…until she's startled by a cell phone ringing.

**

"Call again. Call again!"

"I'm calling, Jordan, just sit down, shut up and wait," his wife argues, strained by the circumstances surrounding her family's life.

"She always has her cell phone on her, Dr. Balentine. Always. The cop just said they didn't see any cell phone on her at all, and that it may be in the house, but … I don't think so. That's like her third arm. There could be information on it."

Dr. Balentine remains silent as he looks up toward the second floor of his majestic home, thinking of the future of his daughter. Then, he looks back down at the congressman as he watches his wife continue to dial the number. An investigator stands by with a cell phone on his ear, waiting on word of the phone in question to be located inside the house or the deceased's vehicle. So far, after three calls and officers scattered about the house, there is no sign of it at all.

"Look, just like we said," Zeena's mother states, slamming her cell phone down, "she wouldn't be that far away from her phone. We know our daughter! There's something wrong. Who was at the party?"

"We're hoping to identify people at the party through any possible cell phone pictures, texts…even social media posts…"

"It's private! We don't know how to see her pictures on there. Everything has a damn passcode!" she screams at the officer who then backs away to talk to her husband who is more in control of himself.

"Sir, the only thing left for us to do is to track her phone. If her location is on and if the phone remains on, it's a sure way to find out where it is and if it is in the hands of the person who was last with her." Congressman Castles agrees to the trace, and then the officer turns to Dr. Balentine. "I understand your daughter was at the party tonight. I would like to speak with her please, sir, only to ask who was there tonight. She isn't under suspicion, but we understand due to the gravity of the situation if…"

"No, no," he responds, weighing the odds of his daughter Alexis handling the interview well. He believes the odds are in her favor if she speaks. "If that's all you want to know, I'm sure she can answer that."

"And just a few other preliminary questions like what time she left and other general items. Feel free to sit with us and your daughter does have a right…"

"I'm aware of our rights," Dr. Balentine interjects. "But I want to help in every way we can. Whatever it is, I'm just a slight bit afraid for my daughter's sake…her identity."

"Absolutely, sir. It will remain private."

"Thank you. I'll get her." Refusing to allow his emotions to override his rationale, he forces the fear of his daughter being arrested to a confident and secure place, and he walks firmly up the staircase toward her bedroom. When he arrives, he knocks and turns the doorknob which is locked.

"Alexis, open the door, please. I need to come inside." When he gets no answer, he adds, "The officer downstairs would like a word with you."

At that, the door opens to Alexis who has already changed her garb from when she spoke with them earlier and learned of the murder, to clothes that she would wear on a quick drive out. Her shoes aren't laced, but she has on a fresh pair of blue jeans with a short sleeve yellow blouse.

"I was already on my way out, so I suppose I will talk." She attempts to walk by him, but he grabs her arm firmly, so firm that when she tries to snatch away, it doesn't work.

"If you want to get out of this, you need to tell *me* everything and *them* nothing important! Just who was there and that's it. Do you understand?" he whispers full of anguish.

"Sure. Is it because you care about your reputation or me?"

Her father doesn't cave to her manipulative guilt-prompting response, but instead brings her closer to his face and sternly says, "Both. You wouldn't have what you have or have gotten away with what you've gotten away with if it wasn't for my money or my reputation. You remember that!" He squeezes her arm harder. "Now do as I say."

He loosens his grip as Alexis stares back at him in shock. Then, she slowly pulls her arm away and walks down the staircase with her car keys in hand as her father follows her down. She observes the investigator as well as Zeena's parents who sit near her mother, and she pauses on the stairs, not willing to speak in front of them. Her dad nudges her forward, and she realizes that she has no choice. She'll do it if she wants to appear innocent. She has nothing against Zeena's parents. The only reason she killed their daughter is because she wants her freedom, and Zeena knew too much about an incident that she believes no one else knows about.

"Alexis? Nice to meet you. I'm Detective Rogue. I need to ask you some questions that could possibly help with the investigation about the death of your friend Zeena."

"Okay," she answers, sitting at a lone chair in the corner. The officer follows her there, and her parents look on anxiously along with Mr. and Mrs. Castles. As she sits, she intentionally looks at the floor, mapping out what she will say and how she will perform for both the investigator and her parents. She is aware that a head that hangs low can be taken for extreme sorrow, so she makes good on it. Finally, she looks up at the officer when he asks two simple questions – what time did she leave and who was there?

"I don't know exactly what time I left, but I know it was before the others. It was around a quarter after ten o'clock or maybe a quarter 'til eleven tonight, I guess. As far as who was there, I don't know them all by name. I can tell you one or two by name, but there were definitely two girls that aren't from around here. I've never seen them before. At the time, they were nice." She glances at her father, and she could tell by his eyes, he wanted her to stop speaking about things she wasn't asked about. However, Alexis has her own agenda he knows nothing about.

"What do you mean, *at the time* they were nice?"

She hesitantly peers up at her mother who seems to be pushing her to talk, and then she explains, "Well, when I brought the pizza in, I got to know one of the girls a little bit as she was with me as we got a slice of pizza from the kitchen. She told me that she wasn't from around here. I didn't think much of it until I offered her a ride home. See, it was her and the person she came with that got into an argument, so I offered to take her home when her friend left her behind."

"What happened after that?"

"As I was going down the road, she told me to make one last turn, and when I did, I realized she was telling me to go into Gabriel's Trails. I pulled to the entrance, and she attacked me."

Alexis' mother and father react in horror and disbelief at the confession that their own daughter was also attacked tonight. Lorah makes a move toward Alexis for comfort and encouragement, however, before she even gets one foot in front of the other, Michael grabs her arm lightly and shakes his head. Then he leans in toward her ear and whispers, "Just let her tell the story with no interruptions. You can tend to her later."

Lorah plasters herself against his arm, holding on tightly, as she watches the daughter she still sees as a helpless baby speak while her husband looks at her in the exact opposite way. He sees her as a killer with a psychological disorder that may be about to reveal itself to everyone if she makes the wrong move.

"How did she attack you?"

"She just starting hitting me, and I had to put the car in park in order to yank apart from the grip she had on my hair. She was pounding me in the top of my head, trying to drag me out of the door…the door on her side. I didn't even know what was going on, but when I got free, I just took off."

"What was her name?" He asks as he turns back to look at not only Alexis' parents but the Castles as well, with an optimistic appearance on his face. He plants the tip of the ball point pen onto his pad and follows Alexis' lips as she utters the name…

"Tryina. Her name is Tryina."

"Was there an argument of some sort that would have led to the violence?"

"No, officer. I was just giving her a ride home. Why she attacked me...you would actually have to ask her." Alexis has no problem telling the officer to question Tryina about it either because no one will ever believe anything she says because of where she is from.

"Thanks, Alexis. I'm sure this information will be valuable." The investigator stands and walks toward both sets of parents while Alexis sits there quietly, watching her father's movements, how he exudes intelligence and wealth while being even more of a deceiver than her. Each time she's around him, she's reminded of that day he called her a whore and how he slapped her in the face years ago without even asking about the motive for her actions. In all her tears, she not only felt trapped but was trapped, and when she needed her dad the most, he only added to her injury inside. She was at her lowest and never proud of what she'd done, but all he could and would think about was himself.

As Alexis continues to sit still, she realizes that her story can easily fall apart. Within minutes or even hours, someone could reveal something that results in her arrest. While she internally suffers from panic, she makes the decision to runaway. When she stands, her mother rushes over to her with a big embrace, tears streaming down her face as if she's the one who lost a daughter. Right after that, Alexis leaves the house, leaving everyone to only assume that it's because she needs a breather. She allows them to assume. Thirty minutes later, she parks outside of a house waiting for her only relief to meet her where she left him.

**

She rubs her hand across the loveseat, the same loveseat where she just shot a man to death in her home, and slides her fingers around the cushions. The ringing from the cell phone has already ended, however, before it stopped sounding off, she noticed the noise was coming from the area where the dead man sat. Her fingers slide down the sides of the cushion until they hit something hard. She pulls it out of the chair, and as she examines it, she notices that it's more than likely a female's phone because of the highly decorated casing it sits inside.

"Another phone?" she asks herself as she begins to tie the phone to her deceased friend Macy. "She didn't even tell me she had another cell phone. Totally different from her other one."

There is a picture of a child on the cell phone's wallpaper, and as she sets her mind on unlocking it, she turns on a light and holds it up to that same light to try and trace the finger movements against the phone lock. It's a square with a line in the middle. She sits the phone on the coffee table, and again, begins to cry as she lowers to her knees and attempts to unlock it.

"You set me up, Macy. I can't believe you set me up," she silently cries. The first attempt on the lock fails. She tries to unlock again, figuring that after three tries, the phone will automatically shut down. "Come on and open," she whispers as she begins again, this time placing her finger to start at the middle line. As she traces around, she holds her breath. When the phone doesn't open, she calls Chief on her phone.

"Chief," she says after he picks up.

"Yeah, talk, but not about that, you understand?" he quickly reminds her.

"Yeah, I do, but…I think she left her phone here. I was trying to open it up, but now that I think about it, should I?"

"A phone? Hell no. Don't touch that shit. I'll be back to get it."

"Apparently, she had two, and I've never seen this one."

"Listen, I'll be back there in about ten minutes…after I handle this link up," he states referring to drugs.

"Hold on for a minute, Chief." She goes silent and listens closely, hearing some movement outside of her home. "Somebody is at my door. I hear something…"

"Tryina," he shouts. "Hide that damn gun! Put it in your brother's room now! Don't turn on any fuckin' lights, and play it cool," he orders her, believing that someone has found Macy and traced the phone to her place.

Ever since her brother was died, Tryina's left his room the exact same way. She speedily listens to Chief, now believing that it may be officers outside her place coming to question her about either Macy or Tony. Quickly, she opens one of her brother's drawers, wipes her prints from the pistol, and closes the drawer back. As she leaves the room, she locks the door behind herself, wipes her face and remembers the unidentified phone which she assumes is Macy's. She picks back up her cell phone.

"Chief, what about the phone?" She listens, but no one is on the other end. "Chief?" Immediately, she wipes the call from her cell phone and as she begins to make her way to the front door, it busts open right in front of her. She falls to the ground in horror as police officers swarm all around her, their guns aimed directly at her skull.

"What are you here for?" she screams, staring straight out into the street where she gets a glimpse of Chief standing directly across the street watching. She knows to keep her mouth closed, or she will never get out.

**

She reaches for her cell phone to call him once more, however, when she looks through the windshield again, she notices a figure coming out from behind the house, causing her to drop her phone back down onto the seat. She turns on her low beams and keeps the car running just in case it isn't the person she wants by her side. As the male approaches, she soon realizes that it is him. Then, she turns her low beams off, and unlocks her door. When he reaches the car, she turns it back on, and he gets inside.

"Wait," he commands, reaching for her hand on the gearshift. "Where are you going?"

"Javis, we have to go."

"Take your hand off the gear, Alexis," he sighs.

"Javis…"

"We don't have to go anywhere," he interjects, staring at his home. "We really don't have to go anywhere, at least not right now." He motions her to turn off the engine. "Leave your car right here. Walk back with me."

"To your house? I can't go in there, Javis… I…" she panics. Just thinking about going any closer to his house, the home she tore apart years back, makes her feel ill. She grabs her stomach. He notices how tense she is, therefore, he gets out of the car, and walks over to her side, opens the car door and takes her by the hand.

"No one is inside," he responds passionately. "Come on with me. It's okay." Holding out his hand, Alexis glances back at the house and then, teary-eyed and afraid to confront anyone in his family, she decides to trust him while lifting her hand to place it inside his. The car's motor silences, and all that is heard between them is their passion for one another. It's not long before they enter his house.

When she walks inside, she scans the place, and it is nothing close to as immaculate as her home, and it seems they have even less than they had when the family lived in Gabriel's Trails. Nothing has a match. There is a sofa, but no loveseat and chair. There are frames snuggling up with photos of his family, and when the family photos seem to corner her mentally, she turns to leave, but Javis stands blocking her path to the door.

"You can leave if you want to, Alexis," he offers, not willing to force her into a decision. However, when she remains silent, he provides a solution for them both. "We just need to let this go...let this happen." Again, he takes her by her hands and draws her closer to him. "I don't have much of anything, even after two years of us being apart, but when I saw you..."

"When you saw me, you knew it wouldn't matter. It didn't matter then, and it doesn't matter now." There is a pause before she continues, "Javis, I'm so sorry." Her eyes meet his as he leans down to meet her in a passionate kiss, one that he's longed to initiate in solitude.

As they kiss, she invites him to remove her shirt by placing his hands underneath, but he doesn't. Instead, he removes his and tosses it over onto the sofa. Then, he picks her up from her thighs, and she straddles him, holding onto him tightly as he walks her gently back to his bedroom. Nothing is prepared for the occasion, but that doesn't matter to either of them as he lies her on the unmade bed. She caresses the back of his neck as he softly kisses her on her face and then on down to her neck. The sensation of his skin on her fingertips begin to soothe the pain she's been in for so long, and it's her soft moans that seduce him, moving him far away from his agony and into a place of finally being understood, desired, and more importantly needed, just like he truly believes she needs him.

They make love under a damaged rooftop and on a bed that sits on an unlevel floor, with an air conditioning wall unit that could be heard struggling to pump a coolness over the warmth given off by their bodies. He turns her naked body over and kisses her all over her back, and as he moves down toward her thighs, he stops as he feels a line of scars. Alexis snaps out of her trance, turning back over, terrified at what she's accidently allowed him to see.

"Javis, it's nothing. It's not what it looks like."

"You do it to make it all go away, don't you?"

"Give me my clothes!" she shouts, full of shame as she moves quickly to leave the room, deeply disturbed by his find. She doesn't make it two feet from the bed before he stops her while she tries to fight free. "Just leave me alone! You don't know what I've done! You just don't know, Javis, so leave me alone. Let me go," she cries, but Javis won't allow her to leave so easily this time.

"Alexis, it can't be any worse than anything I've done."

"You don't know," she responds angrily.

"You won't need to do that anymore," he responds, shifting his eyes to her scarred up inner thigh. He moves her hair away from her shamed, yet beautiful, face. "You can't tell me that you don't need me with you right now, Alexis, because this is the freest I've felt in years. It's easy to want to hurt yourself, but let's make it just as easy to not. Calm down. It's just you and me, and I won't tell."

As he speaks, she believes every word he says, and as his lips come back to meet hers, she allows them to take away her sorrows in hopes that those same sorrows will never return. She finally escapes completely from her mental state and the things that transpired only hours ago, and she relaxes in his arms with a man who she truly feels loves her, no matter what she's done.

As the night progresses, Alexis stares at him while he sleeps. Her hand moves across his chest while he lies on his back with his arm underneath her. Watching him breathe and imagining herself being dishonest with him once again becomes unbearable, believing that it was her dishonesty the first time around that caused things to end so terribly, with irreversible damage. She lifts herself up, and that is all it takes for Javis to awaken from his sleep only to see the young lady he just made love to sitting with her back to him. He reaches to touch her skin, and just as she feels the warmth from his palm against her naked back, she speaks.

"Javis, I killed someone last night, just some hours ago."

"You did what?" he asks, pushing himself away from her to sit erect and try his best to digest what she just said to him. "Alexis."

"What?"

"I just asked you what you said."

Her eyes drop to the white sheets that cover her legs, and she says it once more. "I killed someone. Last night is when it happened."

Javis recalls her crying on the telephone, and how he thought she was crying for her past sins, not present ones. Thoughts begin to rush through his head with hundreds of questions he wants to ask her about what she just confessed, but instead of falling for his heart's prompts, he goes with his mind instead.

"You're not a killer, Alexis. Was it self-defense?"

"Yeah, it was," she answers, grateful for him listening to her and not judging. "She knew something about my previous crimes, and she would have eventually turned me in. I had to kill her."

"Well, I was thinking about what you said," he responds as he sits up, taking hold of her hand. "I can't leave with you, Lex, because my mom. She's extremely sick, and we're out of money. The reason she isn't here right now is because I had to send her back to the hospital. My brother is there with her now. I have to find a way to make more money and as soon as I do, we can leave these troubles. I'm tired, Lex." He leans in and kisses her. "We all make mistakes, and we've both learned that we also have to do what we have to do sometimes."

Alexis reaches over and embraces him while he also holds her in his arms, his thoughts only about financing the future of his family out of a hole of debt and despair that seems to grow bigger and wider.

"I can get you the money. I can get you the money by tomorrow. Whatever it is, I can pay for it through my education fund."

He pulls back from her, caressing her face and wiping her tears at the same time. "Alexis, don't do that. I'll find a way."

"No, this is the easiest way. You're the only one that I trust. You're the only one that's been honest with me in spite of myself. Don't you even want to know?"

Javis assumes she is referring to whom it was she killed, so he pauses for a minute. "I already know. There was a murder tonight in your neighborhood. When you said you'd killed someone, I'd already put two and two together."

"Then I'll get the money. We will always care for your mother, from afar, and your brother. I have enough money all on my own, and there is no way my mother will let me be without. We can leave between now and when I see you again."

"Are you sure?"

"I love you, Javis."

There is a silence that could only bother a woman in love, and that is a man who doesn't return her affection in the way she is giving it. Javis is young, but he knows this much, so he secures their future with the only answer he knows will seal the situation he's in once and for all.

"I love you, too, Alexis."

DECEPTION

AT

GABRIEL'S

TRAILS

III

DECEPTION AT GABRIEL'S TRAILS III

It's one thing to have regrets, but it's another thing to repent when the bodies are stacking up and the drama is spiraling out of control.

In this merciless game of deception, no one knows who to trust, and throughout all the turmoil, there is one person that stands in the middle of it all – Alexis! When having to choose between living her own life or taking the life of someone else so she can be set free, there's only question left to answer – can she live with the deadly consequences?

"Looks like there was a murder out there at Dominion Lakes."

"Oh yeah?" says a paranoid Tryina. She's never been interrogated before by police officers. The closest she ever came to being interrogated was by her own flesh and blood brother, and there was nothing fair about it. She was to either give him the information that he needed or get mistreated until she did. Through all that he put her through, however, she knew deep down her brother would never harm her permanently for any reason. Now, and especially now, the whole arrest leaves her feeling a great sense of paranoia and fear after killing someone, knowing how long she could be put away in prison if someone ever found out.

As Chief drives her down the road, she peers out the window, ignoring anything else that's going on in the car with him. She is aware that he's turning the stations to find something in particular, but she doesn't know what nor does she care. The only thing she wants to do is get out of the car because just seeing him watch her get arrested only makes her wonder if he was the one who had anything to do with those officers busting in on her. She knows what he does for a living, or really, to the living. He kills. He's the number one killer in the Trails now, and that was the only thing he did for the head gangster named Bain before he was laid to rest.

"You have any idea who was killed out there? The word is that you and Macy were seen walking that way around eight or nine o'clock."

The car hits a bump in the road as she ponders over what to say to Chief next. "You sound like the police, Chief. I kept my mouth shut, just like my brother taught me to, so you don't have to worry about that. And as far as a murder, I don't know of any murder. All I know now, from them telling me, is that it was the congressman's daughter, Zeena. Other than that, I don't know."

"That's good, sis," he responds, cracking a sarcastic smile.

"I'm not playing a good game, so I really don't need any back pats, Chief. I'm being serious. Except the ones you execute and my first fuckin' kill, I don't know what you're talking about when you say there was a murder tonight, except what I got from the cops." She pauses and begins to rub her leg, feeling very anxious about what she's about to say next. "It was the dead girl's phone...Zeena's phone. It was inside my loveseat, so they came to *my* place."

Deep down, she feels like she was set up. As she glances down at Chief's hand, she notices his pistol right there beside him. He never leaves home without it, and she knows he'll use it on anyone, including her, no matter what he wants her to believe. Protecting himself over her is the number one priority for Chief, and she can sense it by this cat and mouse conversation he's having. All she knows is that it was either him or Macy that set her up for those cops to come to her home, and now that Macy's dead, she only has one side of the story.

When she left Zeena's house, she was alive. She's never known Macy to be a killer, and it couldn't have been the girl she hit, Alexis, because she'd just attacked her at the entrance of Gabriel's Trails. That leaves only one thing for Tryina to believe – that Chief could have killed Macy and made her believe Tony was breaking in her house on purpose because he'd already killed Zeena for some reason unbeknownst to her, then planted the phone in her home, having gone through all those changes just to collect her money while still holding on to this gangster loyalty code. If she is gone and locked away, then Chief gets everything with no hitches, leaving her to depend on him.

"How did you know to come get me, Chief?"

"Come get you when?" he asks making a sharp right turn.

"Today, at the entrance. You called my phone. I just assumed...I guess I'm just used to you being around and having eyes everywhere. How did you know I was with Alexis? I mean, when you called, I was shaken up a bit from the fight, but you said that you were on your way. I didn't tell you where I was exactly until after you said that, but how did you know to be *on your way*?"

"You know you have a mind like your brother's. But you're just not as sharp with it. I'm two floors ahead, sis. I knew where Alexis was before you did. I knew she would be at a party tonight up there in Dominion Lakes. I knew that girl named Zeena."

Tryina stiffens at the confession and begins to search for somewhere to leap from the car without getting hurt. Trusting him is not an option. "Why didn't you let me in on what was going on? How do you know her?"

"I don't have to let you in on shit, Tryina. Since when do I answer to you, huh, sis? The less you know, the better you are." He pulls into Gabriel's Trails, and Tryina feels that she could be in real danger. "I'm not the one after you, Tryina. Don't let your mind play games on you."

She stares back into his eyes and no longer sees someone who has her back. Instead, she only sees someone who may have set things up to have his back covered. "My mind doesn't play games on me. It sees things for what they are, especially now, Chief. Thanks for getting me out of there."

He nods his head, and as his car continues to hum outside of her home, he says one last thing. "I'm after Alexis, Tryina. This has nothing to do with you. We're on the same team. Don't fuck up. A girl with that much money, you have to be careful where you kill her. It has to be on your turf or no turf. I got word that she was about to come through here, and it was Zeena who told me."

Tryina exits the car and asks one more question. "And Zeena?" she asks to try and find out again if he killed or had her killed.

He shrugs his shoulders. "That's one less dumb broad I have to kill. I didn't kill her. Let me give you a clue though since you're all wet behind the ears and shit. You need to be focused on how those cops know about that assault you got into at the front. Find out who told them that, and you might find out your real enemy. Don't fuck up. Gabriel's Trails didn't do shit to you."

Tryina slams the door and watches Chief drive off. Then, she whispers underneath her breath as the morning sun rises higher in the sky, "I already know who snitched on me. I even know her last name now…thanks to the cops." From there, she walks inside her home, and before going to sleep, she locates a small, red box inside her closet. She opens the box, and pulls out a picture of herself and another female that her brother used to run with until she was banished from the Trails. On the back of the photograph is a telephone number. She takes it to bed with her and sleeps until the evening comes once again, having not slept all night long while in jail. When she awakens, there the phone number is again, staring her in the face, so she decides to use it.

**

"Come here, son, and hold your head still. I don't have all damn night. You wanted these braids, so sit here and take it."

"But, ma, you're pullin' too hard. Feels like you're taking my whole scalp out," the six year old complains as he folds to his mother's orders.

"You heard me. Braids hurt sometimes. Deal with it," she says as she leans over to pick up her ringing telephone. "Hold on a minute," she says, softening her tone up while kissing whom she considers her big little man on the top of his head. He wipes it off as she answers the phone. "Hello?"

"Kaynine?"

"Why?" she questions the caller without hesitation.

"Because I need her."

The voice triggers a still moment with Kaynine as she removes herself from the chair and walks into another room. "I'll be right back, son, and no, you can't go outside. Sit there so I can finish your hair," she orders as she passes all the pictures on the wall that line her short hallway until she goes into her bedroom, locks the door, and sits on her formally made bed with her elbows atop her knees, staring at the floor with the phone pressed against her ear. "And you need me for what?"

"I don't know who else to call. It's Tryina," she answers with her very recent past causing her to voice quiver while she ponders the unpredictable future.

When Kaynine hears the name, she goes for her cigarettes which are located on the nightstand, lights one up, and then blows the smoke into the air softly and calmly. "Somebody got you fucked up, Tryina? I haven't heard from you in a long time, since…"

"I know. Since I saw you at the funeral, and I had to sneak over there to see you because I remember how close you two used to be. The funeral was hard for me, but I know it was just as hard for you, too."

"Yeah," Kaynine agrees, looking away at the window to clear her head of the bad memories. "Anyway, it's good to hear from you, but I know you wouldn't be calling me if you didn't need me."

"But I would be calling you all the time if I knew it was safe to do so, and you know that."

"So why now? Your damn brother kicked my ass out…him and Bain. It's not your fault because you were just a little girl. I don't hold that against you. I still love you. You were, and still are, like my little niece."

"I remember," Tryina responds. "I know you loved me because you loved my brother. I still don't know why you and him…"

"And you still don't need to know. Some things are better left unsaid, especially to people who have nothing to do with it. You need to learn that shit." She begins to fidget with her long nails as the pain of losing a man she cared so deeply for comes back to haunt her heart. "And you're right.

We were best friends, and I loved him a lot, even after the split. But…back to you. Are you coming to see me?"

"I don't know," Tryina responds. "I was arrested."

"For what?"

"For assault."

"On who?"

After a brief but noticeable pause, Tryina answers just to find out of the name is familiar. "On Alexis."

Kaynine puts out her cigarette and sits up taller on her bed. There was a time when Kaynine was within the inner circle that was considered Bain's territory. There wasn't an inch of that circle where she couldn't breathe and make her presence known as long as Tryina's brother had her back. They were like a family, and the trust ran deep. Even though Kaynine and Tryina's brother were best friends, they became lovers at different points in their lives. There was always a certain type of inseparable love between them, and the love was strong, but they never considered themselves a couple. In that, complications began when she became involved with another man. It was a late night…

~

"Come here, girl," Bain said to her after being up all day, and since nightfall came in, he was in and out of consciousness. Kaynine was in the kitchen making some lasagna which just happened to be her specialty, and being that she liked to cook, she felt like they all needed it. She'd hung out with Floss and Bain the entire time, and she was just as beat.

"Come here for what? Man, I'm just as tired as you. I'm about to put this lasagna in the oven, set this timer, and eat," she said, walking out of the kitchen and into Bain's living room when she noticed Floss was nowhere around. She then pulled up her hair into a ponytail, took a sip of some bottled water and then looked at Bain as he slouched on the couch. "You mean to tell me Floss is already knocked out?" she laughed, however, it was interrupted by a yawn. "Oh man, I'm tired…and hungry."

"I said come here."

Startled by Bain's tone of voice, Kaynine immediately became hesitant, and then glanced at the hallway where she knew Floss was probably sleeping in the furthest bedroom. "I'm tired, too, Bain…"

"Kaynine."

She knew better than to respond in any other way than yes to him, and even though she generally always treated Bain like a brother due to her best friend, and sometimes lover, Floss, that night, it was obvious that Bain had other plans with her. Due to her gift of always being able to calm a man down with words and a good tease, she decided to bet on herself and sit next to him without stirring up trouble. Besides, even though he hadn't taken one sip of alcohol since they've been up, he may have just needed a warm body, at least that was what she told herself. Whatever it was, she had to agree. There was no disagreeing with Bain.

"What's going on, Bain? You okay?" she pretended to not be shaken, but Bain saw right through it.

"I saw you look back there down the hallway. You think I'm about to hurt you just because I told you to come here for a minute?"

"Hurt who? Me?" she laughed loudly on purpose in an attempt to awaken Floss. "You know I love both you guys, and you're like a brother because of Floss…"

"You love me because I'm Bain," he interjected, slowly placing a firm grip around her chin with his right hand. "You see all those ladies out there?"

Kaynine harshly stared back into his eyes, not once looking away like most women do when they come in contact with him. She wasn't raised to worship a man with her eyes, no matter how powerful that man was. She learned from her mother to fight, but if she couldn't fight, to take the beating. After surviving the beating, she was to always, as her mother put it, *"stare the mother fucker right back in his eyes, stand tall, and let him watch you walk away just as good as you did before the beating. Just survive! Do all that, but never kiss the ground for any man but Jesus Christ Himself"*. Kaynine's mother wasn't a saint, but she could tell that her mom was struggling to hold on to what sainthood she had left after the world trampled her down to nothing. It was this memory that made Kaynine not fold nor cry in front of Bain, the man that could take her life and think nothing of it. He would even potentially kill Floss, too, a man she cared for so much, and that was the only reason she decided not to fight, but take the beating.

"They belong to you," she answered, referring to Bain's women, never once taking her eyes from his nor her chin from his grasp. "I don't. I ain't never been no whore for you, and never will I ever."

Bain just smiled. "Take your damn clothes off." He released her, but because she knew his commands were just as powerful as a gun to her head, she did exactly what he commanded. Bain made her eat her words that night. She became his very own personal whore while Floss slept.

Everything was over by the time the lasagna was finished. Then, she got up and obeyed her mother. She stood tall and walked away after shedding not one tear. They all sat and ate – her, Floss and her rapist, Bain. It was that night that Bain hated her, for no other reason except that he couldn't break her down. Her mother was right. He won her body, but he failed to take her spirit.

~

"Listen up, Tryina. I know exactly who you're talking about. I might be on the outs, but I stay informed with what goes on in Gabriel's Trails. Do you know where I live?"

"No, all I ever had was this number."

"Remember this address. Don't write this shit down either. You follow me?"

"Yeah, I do."

"Two-eleven Drilldown Avenue. Come to the back of the building. That side of the building is yellow. I'll meet you by that wall. Just stand there."

"When do I come?"

"Now, dammit!" Kaynine hangs up the phone and changes clothes as she stares at herself in the mirror. "It's been a while. That wasn't the call I was expecting, but I knew my day would come, just as clear as day." After sliding a black and clinging outfit on which makes her hips look thinner and thighs appear even more slender, similar to how she used to be before giving birth, she walks out of her bedroom with a new attitude. "Looks like we both have some shit to handle...see how this all plays out. Hey, baby!"

she calls for her son, and he comes running down the hallway while she puts on make up.

"Huh, ma?"

"Run and change clothes. You're gonna go stay with grandma tonight." The last things she lifts besides her keys is a clutch before heading out. In ten minutes, they're pulling up at her son's grandmother's house, and Kaynine hits the automatic locks.

"Hop out."

Kaynine's son opens the door and rushes up the steps to his grandmother's house as she exits the car. It's been days since she's stopped by to see the woman whom she considers her mother since her own mother has been deceased for quite some time. As she traces his steps with her eyes, the door comes open, and it's his grandmother standing in front of the screen. Once she sees the smile on his grandmother's face, she beeps the horn, hops back in the car, and drives back to her own home. As soon as she gets there, she notices the young lady whom is supposed to meet her, standing at the yellow wall just as she was instructed to do.

Kaynine pulls her car around to the front of the building, exits with her clutch and keys, and then walks calmly to the back of the building. When she approaches the side of the red brick that leads to the yellow, she slows up, takes out a cigarette and lights it. After one quick puff, she turns the corner, stands there and admires the young lady who is standing under the night light that was only a child when she got kicked out of Gabriel's Trails.

Tryina wears a solid cotton and lace top and a pair of blue jeans with sneakers that appear like they've never been worn. She doesn't see Kaynine to her left admiring how she's grown up, but when Kaynine begins walking her way, the footsteps get her attention, and she turns to face a woman she hasn't seen in years.

"Hey, lil mama. Would you look at yourself, all grown up with everywhere to go," Kaynine starts with a big smile on her face as she flicks her cigarette to the side. "It's never been good to smoke in front of children."

"Very funny, Kaynine," Tryina responds, happy to see that Kaynine is in good spirits at her arrival. "I'm not a child anymore as you can see."

"I see. And you have a little style there…shoes clean…just like your brother's," she sighs. "I see he taught you that right? Where's my hug?"

Tryina walks over to her, and they embrace like they are blood relatives. Kaynine then takes Tryina's face in the palm of her hands and stares into her eyes. "Your face looks exactly the same. I see your brother all in you, too," she says, sliding her hands softly down the face of the young lady she used to care for years ago.

"You look just how I remember you, too…auntie."

"Oh, I'm still auntie now? That's good, that's real good, Tryina. Make me feel like I'm still special to you while we ride," she says as she starts to walk off.

"I thought we were gonna be here," Tryina asks confused, and not sure if it's safe to bring her back into the Trails. "I don't know if…"

Kaynine turns around with a slight attitude, staring at the ground Tryina stands on and then back up to her face. "You don't know what? You think them motherfuckers in there don't know me? They know me better than you think you know me." Then she smiles at Tryina as she closes the distance between them, placing a devilish expression on her face. "Sweetheart, what the fuck are they gonna say to you if you ride me in there? The last time I checked, you're kinda like one of the next in line. Don't you hold some damn cards? They don't protect your ass for nothing, baby girl." She turns and walks back toward the front of the building, tired of discussing the issue of returning to the neighborhood. "Come on, Tryina," she drags. "This shit ain't that damn scary, and ain't a mother fuckin' woman in that place scarier than my ass. You know that, but then again, you never did know that about me, did you?" she asks rhetorically. When she finally hears Tryina following behind her, she smiles and slows her prance while searching the parking spaces. "Which is your ride?"

"Over here, Kaynine," she sighs, wondering if she's about to make the biggest mistake of Kaynine's life by taking her to a place that she may never exit.

Driving back to Gabriel's Trails, Tryina watches as Kaynine glosses over everything on the inside of her car which looks nothing like the outside. Camouflage is the best kind of lie, and it's the going trend in Gabriel's Trails. It's not the type of camouflage that one thinks of with the military. Instead, it's all about concealing the inside by the outside, and as far as Tryina's car, it looks regular and inexpensive. However, once inside, from the floors to the roof, it's all custom.

"I like it, lil niece. I sure do. My favorite is wood grain. I have it back inside my car, but it can't hold a candle to what you have in here. It's nice. Who helped you do it?"

"Well, it was all my idea, the colors and all. The guys at the shop did it."

"They're still around?"

"Yeah. They listened to what I had to say and gave me a good price, so…"

"A good price?" she exclaims, glaring at Tryina questionably. "You mean free?"

"Free?"

She tosses her cigarette, unbuckles her seatbelt and turns around to face Tryina while both her arms hug the outside of the car through the open window. "You got to fill me in. Just what the fuck did Floss let you in on and what the hell do you think? Don't you know you run this shit? Hell, them dealers out there probably still owe you money, with all that Floss did for them…him and Bain."

"I'm no gangster, Kaynine." Tryina keeps her eyes on the road. "I'm just the sister to one…a dead one," she states, already regretting killing Tony at her home.

"Yeah, one of the worst ones that walked those streets. Those fools are still so far up his ass that they will do whatever you say."

"They don't fear me, Kaynine. You have it all wrong. Chief looks out for me. He's like a brother," Tryina stutters, her eyes tearing up as she convinces herself of what may not really be.

At those words and the sight of sadness in Tryina's eyes, Kaynine puts her arms back inside the car and rolls up the window. "Chief, huh? It's good to have a gunner like that in your corner, so why the tears that you're trying to hide? You fuckin' scared?"

Tryina finally turns into Gabriel's Trails, but Kaynine doesn't take her eyes off of her until she gives her an answer.

"Yes. I think he may have tried to set me up."

Seconds later, Tryina pulls up to her condo, walks around to the passenger's side, and out steps the woman once banished from the Trails for reasons unknown to her. She's unrecognizable to anyone as she takes the curb and looks around at the few people on the street under the night of the evening.

"This place hasn't changed." She tightens the grip she has on her clutch and walks toward Tryina's home. "Same spot, different owner." She moves past Tryina. "Don't wait too long. I don't have the key. You do." At that, Tryina moves past her and unlocks the front door.

As Kaynine walks into Tryina's home, an uneasy and unsettled feeling comes over her. When her feet touch the floor, instead of continuing to walk, she starves them of any further movement. The smell of the home is still the same as when she used to run the streets with Tryina's brother, and just the scent of it interrupts her confidence because it's as if he's still alive.

"Nothing's changed. I sense something in here though," she states, continuing to take in the furniture, walls and even picture frames that still hang side by side of her parents.

"What can you tell?" Tryina asks, placing her keys inside the tray at the kitchen counter.

Kaynine spins around to connect paths with Tryina. "He's still with you. He never left. Ain't that some shit?"

"How would you know that? You just got here."

"I can sense it. It's that death sense. It feels like someone just died in here. You don't feel that shit?"

Tryina glances over at the loveseat where she shot Tony. The chair appears brand new, however, the invisible stain of his dead body still remains in her head. Suddenly, her eyes stumble back upon Kaynine who ducks purposely into her line of vision, noticing something is the matter.

"Hey, answer me."

"No. Feels like the same old spot to me."

"Well, I feel him in here. It's been a long time, but he's here," she responds slyly, cutting her eyes away from Tryina but still paying close attention.

Tryina swallows and pretends that she isn't bothered by what Kaynine just said. The fact is that someone died right there on her loveseat and the fact that Kaynine can feel a presence is enough to make her change the subject.

"But about Chief…"

"Talk to me. Just why on earth do you think Chief is trying to set you up? You can't be damn serious, can you?"

"I'm very serious. Something happened last night that doesn't make sense, and I need you to help me sort it all out. But you can't say anything to…" As Tryina speaks, she's cut short by loud, chaotic banging on her front door. She immediately glances at Kaynine who only takes a seat in the living room calmly as if everything is fine, prompting her to go ahead and open the door. "Kaynine," she whispers in a panic. Just Kaynine's presence alone in the house will more than likely cause trouble, but because the banging on the door doesn't cease, Tryina bolts toward it, opening it as soon as she sees who is outside.

"Tryina, Tryina," the female cries. "Let me come inside. I have something so bad to tell you. I need you to sit down."

Tryina doesn't utter a word. She lets the female inside, and when she shuts the front door to follow the young lady into the living room, she notices the look of horror on the female's face. The young lady turns to face Tryina, but when Tryina does and says nothing back to her, she continues with the reason she's come over.

"Tryina," she continues shakily as she glosses over once again at the lady that sits before her in Tryina's living room. "I need to tell you something."

"Tell her what?" Kaynine instigates after seeing the fear in the lady's face.

The woman buckles at the sound of Kaynine's voice who sits swinging her crossed leg on the loveseat. Kaynine's eyes continue to sting her as she is suddenly unable to finish her sentence. Finally, Kaynine uncrosses her legs and leans forward, as if she could lunge at the female. "You better tell her what the hell you came here to tell her or my ass is gonna be offended as hell. I already feel unwelcome because of your ass."

"Kaynine, I think she just…"

"I've told you about thinking all your life, Tryina. Isn't that why I'm here now? This lady right here, she knows I'm basically your family. Don't you?"

"You know her, Sheena?" Tryina asks puzzled, realizing that she is truly in the dark about much.

At first there is silence, but then, the woman named Sheena finally answers. "I used to know her." As she

119

speaks, her hands are visibly trembling, and Tryina is well aware of it all.

"Used to know me is one thing, but I'm looking you square in the eyes right now. You know me now, too." Kaynine then sits back in the seat, crosses her legs again and then listens with a huge smile. "You can tell her now that we're all caught up."

Believing that Sheena is safe, especially here inside her home, Tryina walks her toward the kitchen counter. Even though Kaynine is one of the roughest women to deal with, Tryina won't be told what to do and how to treat people in her own house, especially if they've done nothing to deserve it. When Tryina walks her over toward the kitchen area, Kaynine only sits back and laughs, tickled at how the girl she knows as her niece has grown into the woman of what used to be Floss' home.

"Go ahead. Talk. It's fine. I see you're upset, Sheena. What's going down?" Tryina asks as if she doesn't already know. Sheena is Macy's next door neighbor. They have often hung out together whenever Tryina would visit, so it isn't difficult to figure out what has Sheena so upset.

"It's Macy."

"What about Macy?" Tryina prompts her, but when the name Macy comes out of her mouth, it reaches the ears of Kaynine, resulting in her leaning forward to try her best to hear. But when she can't get a good grip on the conversation, she reaches for a cigarette, lights, and moves toward the kitchen herself, growing increasingly frustrated.

Tryina notices Kaynine's movement, but grabs Sheena's hands. "You have got to tell me. What about Macy?"

"She's been killed, Tryina. She was shot. I went over there. I went just now, and the door was open…I mean, unlocked. I don't even remember. But I walked in and saw her on the floor, blood and all," she cries as she falls over into the arms of Tryina. However, when Kaynine hears the situation, she cuts her eyes to the floor, takes three more quick, nervous puffs of her cigarette, and quickly moves back to the loveseat, this time, rocking back and forth while shuffling her eyes everywhere but at the two in the kitchen. "I'm so sorry, Tryina. Did you even know?" Then she whispers, "I'm the one who called the cops. I didn't leave my name, and I just left my place, figuring the cops would stop by and question me, and I'm scared…"

Tryina has nothing to say, so she shields her knowledge of the situation by hugging Sheena and pretending to cry. "I haven't spoken to her all day."

"She looked like she's been dead now for a while. Who would kill her? What did she do?"

"I don't know," Tryina says, moving away from her to place her head on the counter, still shielding true feelings of rage toward the girl who betrayed her. "Thank you, Sheena. I'll call you."

"If you need anything…"

"Yeah. Okay," she responds still in character.

Sheena then rushes out of the front door away from Tryina and most of all, Kaynine. It's not even a minute later that she is on her cellular phone sending word out that Kaynine is back inside Gabriel's Trails, in hopes that the word lands in the right ears.

**

Javis scans the news reports as fast as he can on social media from Alexis' phone while she's in the shower. Although he remained calm on the outside when she revealed to him that she killed someone just last night, inside, he is truly a wreck. Every time he scrolls through the news, he glances up at the bathroom door, believing that she may come back out and see him checking the phone. Finally, he runs into it.

"Congressman Castles?" He sits the phone back down on the bed after reading what the news article had to offer which is far less detailed than what Alexis has already told him. Then, he stares at the bathroom door after exiting out of his social media account and clearing any trace of his searches. He stands up, retracing everything they'd done as soon as they got into the house, then he finally looks up and runs to the window. Her car is parked down the road, and it's been there the whole time. She stayed at his house all day, and now that the evening has set back in, he's suddenly relieved that she parked where she did. His heart pounds heavily as he turns to face the bathroom door once again. Walking over to it, his mind wanders off, trying to figure out if there is another reason why she feels so drawn to him. Was he being sucked in once again and will the blame for the murder land on him?

He places his hand on the door and listens as the water turns off and she steps from the tub. Although it feels like ages before she steps closer to the bathroom door, his eyes are prompted to move toward the door knob after several minutes, and he watches it as it turns. When the door opens, she's startled by him standing there at the door like he's seeing a ghost.

"Javis?" She stands there much thinner in frame than when he first met her while her overall appearance is more mature while downtrodden in obvious ways around her once jovial eyes. Where it was once easy for her to smile, that smile has been replaced by glimmers of wishes and unanswered prayers. However, she is still beautiful in a line of beauties to Javis although he is the only one aware of the destruction that lies beneath her skin.

"Yeah," he responds, well aware that he may not be able to hide his skepticism of her intensions much longer. "You didn't tell me it was Congressman Castles' daughter."

"I didn't think it mattered whose daughter. It was somebody. Besides that, I didn't want you to know the name," she states, moving toward him in an attempt to pass, and he allows her.

"Why not?"

She pauses her gait but doesn't turn around. Her eyes shift to the left and downward and then she answers, "I don't want you to get involved. I was honest with you this time, about everything. The only thing I left out was a name...that I guess you got from my phone."

"I checked my social media account, and there it was. I didn't go through your phone at all..."

She turns around to face him. "I have nothing to hide. You can take my phone whenever. I had a feeling you would want to look, so that's why I left it out here with you anyway." Javis only stands there, unsure of what to believe, and Alexis knows it. Therefore, she removes her towel, allowing it to fall to the floor. "I have nothing else, Javis. I have nothing else to hide."

He holds his breath and walks over to her as she stands there before him unashamed, unafraid and unclothed. Then, he leans over to her ear as if he doesn't even want the walls to hear what he has to say.

"I hope not." He leaves her standing there naked as he goes to shower before they both leave the house in different automobiles, one person going to the hospital and the other going to get the money owed to the hospital. When Javis arrives at the hospital, he walks into the room to his sleeping mother, but his brother is nowhere to be found.

"Mom," he calls at her side while kissing her hand. "Mom, it's me, Javis."

She awakens in a horror, screaming uncontrollably like she normally does when she can't find her children. "Where's Joseph? Where is he?"

"Mom, Ma! Quiet down. Wasn't he here today afterschool? It's way past time."

"No, no, Javis. You don't understand. He didn't ever come back. I'm not crazy. He wasn't here?"

Javis stands up and walks away from the bed frustrated. "What do you mean he never came back?"

"He's not here I said!" Her voice echoes through the hospital's hallway as he moves toward the window, pulls back the curtain and sees nothing but darkness.

"I'm going to find him, ma. He's alright. Let me go find him, okay?" he states fighting to remain calm. This isn't like his brother to go missing ever. Therefore, Javis kisses his mother on the cheek, tells her he loves her, and darts from the hospital room, only stopping to use the phone that is located on another floor of the hospital's waiting area. He calls Alexis, but she doesn't answer.

**

"I do?"

"Yes, dammit, you do have to tell me where you were all night and day long, and you will tell me right now. I had those people in my house all night through today, and they just left! Your mother was worried sick, and don't tell me you didn't check your phone," Alexis' father shouts as he watches her collect much of her apparel to place in a bag.

"I don't have to tell you anything," she pauses as she turns to face him. "Anymore."

At that he storms toward her and throws the clothing from her hands, only to shove her to her own bed. Alexis becomes horrified at the appearance of her father's flustered and demented appearance as he exalts himself over her. She pushes herself further away from him, watching his bloodshot eyes tear through her.

"Do you know what I've done for you already? You think it's just money that you've taken from me, huh? You've taken my peace of mind! That lady…that lady that you thought you killed a couple years back…the one that you left for damn dead, Alexis, and thought only you knew about it? Well she wasn't dead! She showed up at my damn hospital, and I was the fuckin' doctor who released her. Me!"

A shocked Alexis doesn't know how to respond, but her memories go back to the day she left the woman who attacked her in the garage at the side of the trails. All this time she thought she'd murdered that woman. "She wasn't dead? What are you saying, dad?" Suddenly, a surge of guilt takes over her mind as she thinks about how she killed Zeena to cover up what she thought was one of her own deadly past sins.

"I'm saying that you need to tell me…"

"Dad, what are you saying?" she screams with tears already streaming down her face. "You mean you knew about that lady, and you never told me you knew about…"

"There was nothing to tell!" he answers, covering up his own secrets with the woman about whom he speaks. "I paid her. I offered her money after she…she noticed my name," he stutters, "Only after she gave me details that described you and how you look. It was just like she was taking her description of you from a damn picture. She even knew your name, even figured out that you were my daughter. Therefore, I paid her to keep quiet about that other fuckin' murder you committed, which your own story corroborated, and then I told her to leave town. She blackmailed me, and I had to give her money which I knew," he shouts as he points to his chest, "I just knew she would ask for again, month after month. So I had her killed. It took care of everything…our money and you. Now don't fuckin' think you don't owe me a bit more respect than what you already give me. I cleared everything up for you, and I need to clean this up as well, so talk!"

Alexis' head hangs low as she moves to the edge of the bed, slowly continuing to slide her clothes into the bag. Although her dad stands next to her, she feels that there is a huge brick wall there, in between their closeness, that won't ever be torn down. The older she gets, the thicker and taller the wall becomes, until nothing he says penetrates.

Something has finally given her a way out, and she's going to take it.

"I don't need to talk to you, dad. I need to leave." She then looks at her father with barely any compassion, regardless of the story he just fed her about his murder for hire. Since he confessed that he did it for her sake, then that's what she will take. She will take it all for her sake and her sake alone. "I need to leave," she continues softly. "And you're going to give me the money that I need, for as long as I need it."

His face collapses as he moves backward in silence, realizing that his own daughter is betraying him. "Excuse me?"

"You did hear me, didn't you?" she asks calmly.

"I'm not giving you a dime!"

"Sure you will...*dad*," she stresses, lifting her bag from the bed. "Right now, I need all the money you have in your safe. I'm leaving town." She walks closer, unafraid to confront him at this point. "And don't try and murder me because the evidence will be in your own house. I guess I'm not that bad a person after all. Apples and trees, right, dad? You only cloak your bad better."

"You really think you can get away with this?"

"Sure I can. You murdered someone, remember? You tell on me. I tell on you. Her name was Faye, right? That whore?"

Mentally and emotionally disturbed by Alexis' words, Dr. Balentine moves slowly from her bedroom, still in shock about what his own daughter is doing to him, and within two minutes, they are at the safe. Dr. Balentine's own daughter holds him up with blackmail while he has nowhere to turn but where she orders him to go. When he hands her the money, all twenty thousand, she shoves it into her bag while her dad stands stiffly there like she has him held at gun point.

She places the bag on her back. "Move around, dad. Loosen up. This is your house. Transfer some more into my bank account so this will all look natural, and it I'll need it every month…because guess what else I know. I know you've been fuckin' around behind mom's back, too, for years now." She turns and walks off, only looking back to stab her father once more with her sharp tongue. "You were probably fuckin' Faye, too, just like Bain was doing."

Dr. Balentine's face turns pale, so pale that it's clear that he needs help standing. Placing his hand against the safe door, he leans into it, causing it to shut, and he watches his only child leave from his presence, taking his pride with her as she waits for an answer. When she gets none, she digresses.

"I thought so. See, dad. I've learned a lot in the past couple of years." When she makes it to the garage door, she loosens the strong grip of spite for her dad and relieves her emotions in the sadness of her tears. Finally, she looks up at the garage walls and whispers, "I love you, mom." She backs out and goes to prepare for her departure from her side of Gabriel's Trails her own affluent neighborhood, Dominion Lakes. As she travels down the street, she sees that she's been left a voicemail. Lifting her phone to view the recent calls, it's an unidentified number. Instead of calling back, she listens to the voicemail. It's Javis.

**

"Close that shit up, and let's head out there now."

The driver shuts the door. Chief sits in the passenger's seat while a man with a loaded weapon has it pointed directly into the gut of the male sitting beside him in the back seat. The male is quiet, unable to make one sound because he's fear stricken, and when the car begins to move once again, he realizes he's going the one place he's been told never to go ever again.

As the car moves further towards the blanket of trees, he notices that the area has been cleared, so much so that it looks like a ghost town. Unlike the people who are outside at night like usual in the neighborhood, this particular area adjacent to the wooded trails that lead to the next neighborhood is silent and still, causing the male to slowly lose sight of everything he has been taught. He just wants to get away.

"Let me go."

"You remember that fire, big man?" Chief asks the young man they snatched off the street prior to him catching the city bus to get back home. "I'm talkin' to your ass. Answer."

The guy says nothing, regardless of how threatening the situation is getting for him. Silent prayers are sent to heaven with every second that goes by, and he is looking for at least one opportunity to try and get away. His face is bruised and bloody after having been beaten in an empty condo inside Gabriel's Trails, the place he hasn't set foot into since he left. Regardless of where he is right now, the only peace he finds is that one that is inside his spirit, having been raised a strong Christian while not allowing anything or anyone to shake his faith. He's already been through the worst of anything imaginable, and it's going to take more than a threat to scare him because that from the time he could walk, he was already challenged.

Chief laughs at the young man's dissidence and proceeds even further with the story of a fire that he knows has struck a nerve with his backseat passenger. "I set that shit. I watched your limp ass try to save your brother, too. I couldn't come back to finish the damn job with my partners because people would have already called the law on my ass for setting that shit ablaze. I admit, I usually set my shit up better than that, but your brothers' asses had it coming. They killed my partner."

The young man flinches, casting a strong, yet momentary, look at Chief as he sits in the front seat cockily smiling. "*They* never killed anybody a day in their lives," the young man replies as he thinks back to the day his brother was killed. They were both underneath the bed hiding, and it was then that his brother began to ask for forgiveness. It was at that time that he confessed, also. "The person you are after is already dead. You killed him, didn't you? My brother's dead, so isn't that enough?" he shouts.

"The person? It wasn't just one person. In case you didn't know, that fuckin' oldest brother of yours was with him," he says, carving more of a dagger into the young man's heart while twisting his body around to enjoy his passenger's uneasiness. "By the looks of it, you didn't know that shit? When you think about it, your oldest brother is the same mother fucker that got that daddy of yours shot, isn't it? Following behind that rich ass girl. You don't know shit. I don't even want you dead…Joseph. Yeah, I know your damn name. The Moores family. Those who I hit, I know, but that was a long time ago. I'm in a better position now to call all the shots."

"What are you saying about Javis?"

"I'm saying…that shit wasn't an accident. What the hell kind of man sleeps with the woman who had his family killed? Oh you didn't know they were just together last night. Yeah…they were. Naïve ass. I know everything…hell…and this morning. They're probably still together now, shit."

Joseph seethes inside as he goes into deep thought about what Chief just told him, recalling just a couple evenings ago when he stood at the screen door of his home watching Javis there with a young lady. He wasn't certain who it could have been, but he figured the same exact thing that Chief just stated. It was Alexis.

After leaving the house to go spend the night with their mother at the hospital, it all proves to make sense what Chief is saying because Javis would have been alone all that night. Knowing this is when Joseph's thoughts start to spiral out of control while he asks himself many questions, one of which deals with his mother and if she is up there right now alone due to his brother frolicking around with the girl who started the destruction of his family.

As he sits there in silence, making certain he doesn't mumble one thought out loud, the man known as Chief begins to speak to him again. "I figure, if we draw your brother, he'll draw Alexis back in here, too."

"How are you gonna call him? We're broke. He doesn't even have a cell phone, and since you know everything else about him, you should know he isn't at home right now." He glances out the window. "At least he shouldn't be."

"We'll wait."

Joseph knows that it will be impossible to connect with Javis. No one calls him, nor does anyone call the home phone. The other reason why they both stick close to their mother is not only because she goes crazy when they aren't around, but because if something does happen to her, they can be contacted. A home phone isn't that reliable when no one is ever there, so they both opt to take turns with her, basically living at the hospital. Joseph knows the hospital room number but he doesn't dare reveal the location of his mother to the gangsters that have kidnapped him off the street as he left school.

"I have an even better way. You won't have to wait."

The betrayal he feels from his brother's actions, all going on behind his back, starts cutting him to his heart. The thought that he's been dragged into the insanity while being beaten bloody causes a fierce anger to grow against his brother, until he contemplates handing him over. It's becoming obvious that he cares more about himself and Alexis than anyone else. Everyone would be alive if it weren't for them. Then he thinks about his mother. He won't lose her behind his games with a female that helped destroy the only family he has ever had.

"What way is that?"

"I have a number. I memorized it. Send whatever message you will send there, and I'm sure someone you have been looking for will come. You just have to make the message good enough for her to meet you there. It's Alexis. It's her number."

"Hey," he calls Joseph to make him turn and face him. "You think Alexis loves that man…your brother I mean?"

Joseph shrugs. "I guess, man." Before he knows it, there's a bright flash that catches his eyes, causing him to squint and realize at the last minute that his picture is being taken.

"Well, this shot of you and your face all fucked up will send the message loud and clear, or your ass will take their places." The car door opens. "Give me the number."

**

Pulling into the hospital parking lot, she finds a place to park almost immediately. She's well aware of the fact that Javis isn't inside the hospital based on his voicemail, but she is to remain in place until he returns. While she sits inside her car, she begins to count the windows on the outside of the hospital until she reaches the floor that he said his mother was on. That's when she feels the overwhelming sensation to get out of the car. She needs to apologize. It's something she's never done for the mistakes she's made that resulted in so much devastation. She exits her car, taking just her keys and identification.

Her heart pounds harder than her feet pound on the pavement. What once felt like soft, curly hair on her back now feels like the beating of interwoven switches attacking her skin for the crimes that she's committed. Even the breath circulating through her nostrils feels like the stolen travels of dead men. Alexis walks in the guilt of her being while her mind constantly tells her that it's almost over. She's about to leave and never return, but she has to at least leave her trail of apologies to the one that seems most devastated by it all.

With her head down, she walks through the automatic doors of the hospital and recalls the room number that Javis left on the answering machine. When she lifts her head slightly, she notices the elevators, which are directly in front of her, open, and she rushes inside. It's completely empty. From there, her left index finger presses the numerical value for the floor to which she's headed, and instead of lifting her hand from the button, like it is being overpowered by a heavy

133

weight, it slides off of the button slowly, tipping the button beneath it.

The elevator stops briefly to load more passengers while Alexis moves further to the back wall, making eye contact with no one. She feels out of place, yet needed…emotional, but determined. Finally, as she reaches the floor and moves past the people in front of her to approach the double doors, she realizes she is no longer in control. Panic strikes as her mind stumbles over everything that has happened, but she quickly pulls herself back together when the double doors open from the other side, allowing her to walk in as a male nurse walks out. She passes by a vacant nurses' station to head down to the room that's on the end of the hallway. She stalls briefly before entering.

There she is. The woman that she only saw face to face a couple of times looks like she's aged more than the couple of years than they've been separated from each other. She's sleeping, lying comfortably on her back while her head is elevated on a white pillow while the sheets only cradle her legs. Alexis moves into the room as quietly as she can and takes a seat in a brown recliner next to the bed. Then, she speaks.

"Mrs. Moores? Do you hear me? Mrs. Moores?"

Expecting a nurse, Mrs. Moores awakens slightly confused as to who is sitting next to her in a chair. She sits up immediately, and stares at her until it's obvious who the young lady is.

"Get out," she calmly states in disbelief of how the young lady is comfortable sitting in her presence. "I've already heard about you…"

"I will leave," she interrupts. "I'll leave as soon as I'm finished telling you that I'm sorry. I'm sorry for deceiving your family, like I didn't know anything about why I'm accused of causing what's going on…"

"Accused? You get out of here, and leave my family alone."

Alexis abruptly stands up. "I didn't want you to hear that I'm sorry from anyone else but myself because I'm going to be with Javis from now on. I've brought the money to pay your bills. I love him, and we're leaving for a while. I have so much money you won't have to worry…"

"You won't take my son anywhere. You hear me? That's my son. You've already taken everything away from me, now you just get out. Javis will never leave my side unless I let him. I gave birth to him," she promises, leaning over until she's face to face with whom she sees as a demon. "And it will be over my decaying body before I just give him to you. You didn't have power over him then, and you don't now. I raised him!" She raises her voice to a pitch that ends up being met with a teary eyed and horrified Alexis who fears losing everything that she wants to fix, so much so that she suddenly slams her hand around Mrs. Moores' nose and mouth and with her other hand places a choke hold with her other arm around her neck. The strikes being thrown back at her only make contact with her shoulders and arms, creating red whelps that don't break the skin.

As Alexis' strength begins to dissipate, she notices that the heavy hospital door is cracked slightly. Therefore, she gives Mrs. Moores' neck a hard squeeze, cutting off her oxygen. Then, she drags a portion of Mrs. Moores' weak yet fighting upper body off the side of the bed between the rail and the headboard. Mrs. Moores is stuck, gasping for air against the bar.

"Just listen to me, Mrs. Moores. I need Javis with me. I'm going crazy inside…please! You're right he won't leave with me if you say no to him," Alexis pleads as Mrs. Moores' body goes limp. "That's why I can't let you. He loves you too much."

Finally, Mrs. Moores body drifts into lifelessness , prompting Alexis to drop her hands from around her. The sheets are already jumbled, so she rips a sheet from the mattress, ties it around the woman's neck, and rolls her body to the edge of the bed. In the end, she shoves Mrs. Moores' body over the rail, causing it to collapse to the floor, her neck dangling from the bed rail. Alexis stands back, and then apologizes once more.

"I'm sorry."

Her hands shake as she walks to the room door, and when she doesn't hear any footsteps, she peers through the crack that's left in the door. As she steps out, she doesn't go back toward the elevator. Instead, she turns right and takes the stairs. It takes several minutes for her to get to the car, and as she goes to open the car door and climb inside, she reaches inside her purse and pulls out a small razor. Her hands begin to tremble, and she starts to stomp the floor of her car in terrific emotional pain.

"No!" she screams as she bangs the steering wheel until finally, she rolls her window down and throws the razor into a set of bushes that trail the sidewalk between the parking spots. "Come back, Javis. Come back," she weeps.

**

Sweeping the streets from the high school to the neighborhood, and even rechecking the house, Javis finds Joseph nowhere around. His anxiety builds, and his worry escalates to a point that he can no longer think straight. Something has happened, and he knows it. Joseph can't walk long distances, so this isn't like him to up and leave.

"Dang, man, not now. Not now!" he shouts as the gas hand drifts even closer to empty. "I can't believe this," he complains, rolling down the window to shout in desperation. "Joseph!" He views that gas hand once again and realizes that he needs to get back to the hospital because he is completely out of money. "Please be back at the hospital. Just be back there. I need you there."

His mind starts to escape him as terrible thoughts bombard every corner of his brain. A migraine ensues, and with each turn back to the hospital, the throbbing in his head creates an impossible pain in his vessels that he can't ignore. Reaching into the glove compartment, he shoves everything out in order to see if there is any medication. Unfortunately, there isn't anything inside but an old driver's manual, comb and brush, scraps of paper and a pack of pens. He slams the glove compartment back, and then continues on his way to the hospital in hopes that Alexis is already there.

"I need some money," he mumbles as the stress he's under makes way for tears that overpower him as he takes on the blurriness of the street. There's a slight traffic jam before he has to take another turn, so he sits there in his undying sorrow waiting for relief, beginning to imagine his youngest brother being dead somewhere while there is no way to contact the next of kin. He starts to think that maybe he should go back to the house and wait on him, but then again, maybe the hospital is the only place to wait, just in case they bring a body in. Being haunted by his past losses, Javis is broken from his nightmares when he hears car horns blaring behind him. The noise jerks him into action, and he pulls himself together with the knowledge that he can't allow himself to be broken down by thoughts that have the potential to destroy faster than a bullet.

It's not long before he pulls into the hospital parking lot in search of a fast park so he can run up to the hospital room to check on his mother and, hopefully, find his brother. As he circles the lot, he notices a female waving her arms wildly. He stomps the brakes, and turns the car around, rushing to her as fast as he can without hitting a pedestrian and causing more harm than any good. Turning on the emergency lights, he hops out of the car after stopping in the middle of the aisle and runs toward her.

"Have you seen my brother? Do you remember my younger brother?" he asks her.

Alexis stares back confused but answers, "No. No…nobody. I was sitting in the lobby, and didn't see anyone remotely similar to him. I just came back out…like you told me to wait. I… I even walked up and peeked inside the room, but nobody was up there. I just came down," she pauses, "Just now."

"And you didn't see anyone?"

"No. No one."

Javis looks back at his mother's car and then glances up at the hospital room window. Then, he takes his attention back to Alexis. "I know we had a plan, but my brother's missing. I don't know where he is, and I'm running out of gas, and…"

"Well, let's go find him. We have time. I have the money we need and all that for your mother and…"

"Well money isn't gonna fix my situation if I don't find my brother. She needs him, and I need him, too. He's the only brother I got left. I can't go back up to her room without him. It won't be good, Alexis."

"We'll find him. Let me back out, and you pull your car in right here. Then, you take the wheel because you'll know where to look, right?"

"Yeah, cool," he says as he hops back inside his car, still searching for anyone walking who looks remotely like his brother. As Alexis pulls out her car, he takes the parking spot. Finally, as she stops her car and scoots over, he runs around to her automobile, slides into the driver's seat and takes off. "Let me use your phone."

"Here."

"I can at least call the home phone to see if he's there without having to drive over there. That's one thing I need...my own cell phone."

"We'll get one," Alexis responds, ready to take not only his mind off of worry but make him feel like she is all he needs. "And everything will be fine. No matter what," she continues with the dead face of Mrs. Moores in the back of her mind. "Everything will be okay."

As he drives, he dials. When the phone rings, that's all it does is ring, causing Javis' emotions to worsen. "If I don't find him, we can't go."

"We'll find him." As she speaks, she watches a message come through on her phone while he's holding the phone directly above the steering wheel about to dial his home once again. "Let me see that," she asks, reaching for the phone. He hands it to her and watches as she opens up the message. "I don't know this number." She touches the digital envelope only to see a gruesome picture of a young man, seated in a car, with a bruised face. Shaken about the text, she contemplates not showing the message to Javis as it is addressed to him, but when Javis sees the horror in her face, he questions it.

"What?"

"It's for you," she answers hesitantly. "Javis…I don't know what's going on. I don't know…"

"What?" he says, slowing the car down and glancing closer at the phone. It's at that time that he sees a familiar face, but the face isn't like he knows it to be. It's torn and bruised. Snatching the phone from Alexis, he pulls the car over into the bus stop area, and as everyone at the bus stop stares on confused and waving him away, he grips the cell phone in disbelief. Then, he looks at Alexis. "Who sent this?" he shouts. "Dammit, who sent this message, Alexis? You know where my brother is and didn't tell me? You set me up?"

"No! No, I don't know. They must know we're together somehow because they're sending it to me, like he's my brother!" She searches around outside through the window, looking for anyone at the bus stop texting with a cell phone.

"They? Who the hell is they? Look at my brother's face!"

"I don't know!"

"They have my brother. The message says come get him. How the hell am I supposed to know where? You must know."

"Javis, listen to me. I don't! Message the number back. Just…" She snatches the phone and texts a response that reads *where do I come get him*? They both wait for about two minutes before another text comes through. The tension is brutal, and the anger that grows inside Javis for Alexis worsens with every second there is no response. Before Alexis can even read the responding text, Javis snatches it from her hands and reads it himself.

"At the same place you killed Bain."

The message lands on Alexis' ears like a roaring freight train, and she starts to tremble, realizing that she's about to be killed. "No, no…I'm not going." She unlocks the door.

"Don't open this car door, Alexis. If we are going to be together," He reaches out to hold her wrist. "Then, we are in this together. Isn't that what you wanted?" he asks, making up a reason to hold on to her and her money.

Fearfully, she removes her hand from the car door. "It's what I still want," she answers while staring at the dash board. Visions of killing his mother flash before her eyes, and she feels death has finally come for her. Guilt overwhelms her, but not as much as her desire to run away with him. She'll do anything, and she believes in her life with Javis so much until she agrees one more time. "I do. I'm with you."

"Well take me to the spot…the spot where you killed Bain."

As Alexis directs him back to Gabriel's Trails, it is back at the hospital where the staff discovers Mrs. Moores' lifeless body hanging from the bedrail.

**

"What's wrong with you?" Kaynine asks after a long ten minutes of Tryina not speaking at all after the horrible news of her best friend being killed came to her doorstep.

"What do you mean? My friend just got killed…and I'm just now finding out about it."

"Tryina, I'm not a dumb ass," she responds, taking a deep breath while moving slowly toward the entrance of the foyer to ensure that the front door was completely shut. "Your friend is dead, and that fake ass emotion isn't gonna cut it." Then she continues to inspect Tryina like a mortician examines a body, studying every inch of her face and how she is presenting herself.

Terrified that Kaynine has already read her like an open book, she doesn't respond at all to the insinuation. Instead, Tryina allows her eyes to fall to the floor before regaining the confidence that she's going to need in order to play the role of innocent. However, none of it works, and she realizes that as Kaynine speaks again.

"You're not me, Tryina. You never were me, and you can't fool me. Your damn brother never wanted you in these streets, and he thought he was gonna live forever," she rambles, walking over to Tryina in order to get a better look at her, "Until somebody took that fantasy from him."

At those words, Tryina cringes slightly, and Kaynine catches her in the action. Smiling, Kaynine reaches over and pats the back of Tryina's hair. "You see that, what you just did? That's a natural reaction to someone who lost someone that was connected to their heart." Kaynine, then, positions her face directly in front of Tryina's. "You knew your friend was dead because you barely reacted to the news. You even know who did it, don't you?"

Their eyes meet, and layers of lies formulate beneath the surface of Tryina's lips. Before she is able to set them free, her cell phone rings, causing Kaynine to disengage and glance toward Tryina's pocket. Tryina doesn't answer fast enough, so Kaynine reaches for the cell phone herself, but that triggers fright inside the young lady whom she considers a niece, causing her to grab the phone first.

"Hello?"

"Bring your ass to the trails. Trail number two. I got somebody waiting on you. Maybe your young ass can then tell real from fake." The phone hangs up, but before it hangs up, Kaynine snatches it long enough to hear a boastful laugh on the other end. It's a laugh that she's heard before numerous times, and she knows exactly who it is.

Tryina doesn't try to wrestle the phone back from Kaynine because she knows it will be a lost cause for her. Instead, she ends up swallowing the cold truth, and that particular truth is that she may have made the wrong move by calling on Kaynine, not because she doesn't trust her, but because once Kaynine is involved in anything, most of the time, there is always a finish. Tryina already knows it's too late.

"What does Chief want with you?" she asks curiously, but confidently.

"He wants me to meet him somewhere."

"Why?" she continues to press for information.

"Because he just does," Tryina responds, annoyed and wondering why Kaynine is pressing her so hard.

"Are you going?"

"Do I have a choice?"

143

"Hell yeah. Fuck him. His ass is gonna kill you. Where did he tell you to meet him, baby niece?"

"The trails."

"Has he ever in your life told you to come out there?"

Tryina's eyes tear up. "No."

"Damn right. I know some shit you don't know. This man right here is setting you up. Remember your gut? It feels, too, and most of the time, it's right. Either way though…you're a dead girl, and his hands are gonna be clean. He killed your friend, didn't he?" Tryina doesn't answer, so Kaynine answers for her. "Who the hell are you protecting?" she yells. "Grow the fuck up, baby. Everybody ain't your friend…and everyone isn't your enemy. Chief isn't either one. He just does what he has to do, or what he feels he has to do, to get a job done, even if he's paid to do it. What does he feel he has to do to you, Tryina?"

Like a little naïve girl, she stands there silently, afraid of her own words in her own home. Every ounce of confidence and anger she had yesterday has diminished and transformed into fear and confusion, just like a child who is left at school for the very first time amongst strangers although she's lived around the school all her life. Tryina may have grown up around the streets, but this is her first time actually being placed inside the life of them, having to do what is necessary to only live. Even though she'd stood right there in her living room and shot a man to death and even attacked Alexis, her knees buckle at the thought of going against Chief who is a real killer by nature.

"I heard him on that phone. I heard the whole thing. Take me with you." Tryina doesn't move. "Girl, wake up!"

"I am awake!" Tryina shouts back. "Stop yelling at me! You don't know what I had to do…"

"Forget what you had to do. I don't even give a damn about it. It's never about what you *did*. It's always about what you have to do out here. Forget what anyone has ever done for you because that shit can change instantly, Tryina."

"Have you ever killed somebody?" she retorts angrily back at Kaynine.

"Fuck what I've ever done. I wouldn't say if I did anway. A better question is, would I do it?" Kaynine asks so close to the skin on Tryina's cheek that she can smell the odor from the morning's lotion application. "Is that the question you're asking me? Will I do it?" Kaynine steps back and waits, never removing her eyes from Tryina's face.

"If he's gonna kill me…how…" Tryina starts, troubled by every thought and word, so Kaynine volunteers.

"I will. I will kill him before he gets to you. He doesn't know I'm here. Take me with you. What trail is he on?"

"Number two."

"Good. Drop me in Dominion Lakes, and I'll walk through. Don't fuckin' move a muscle near me if you hear me. I'll take the shot." She falls silent and watches Tryina's breathing. "You made the right call by getting me. You need me, Tryina, and like I've always told you, I'm there for you." She walks over to grab her clutch from the living room quickly and snaps her finger to break Tryina's fearful trance. "When you drop me off, drive slowly. Park your car away from the trails somewhere. No one is gonna snitch on you if they see anything anyway. They're afraid of you but more of who you come from. Walk in that trail and plan on walking out alive. I sure as hell am. Go along with whatever he says, and I'll do the rest."

"What if we're wrong?" Tryina asks, fully aware that her actions may get her life in prison or even death if things don't go as planned. Harboring the secret of her previous killing isn't helping because if Chief's running partners ever found out she was in on having Chief killed, then it would mean her own life or they would do something as simple as snitch to the cops. Her life would be over either way.

"I'm never wrong. I'm fuckin' Kaynine."

DECEPTION

AT

GABRIEL'S
TRAILS
IV

DECEPTION AT GABRIEL'S TRAILS IV

When the walls are caving in, and the smell of death looms overhead, the many deceivers of Gabriel's Trails are left to come face to face with their dead.

After a young lady determines that her own life should be spared, desperately, she makes the wrong turn, and ends up in the trails. When bodies start to fall, her own life flashes before her eyes as trust betrays her, guiding her directly into her demise.

"Mrs. Moores? Mrs. Moores, can you hear me?" the nurse asks, her pulse rising as she unravels the sheet from the woman's neck. The blood has already ceased from flowing to her lips, and it's evident to the nurse that if she doesn't act fast, there may be no reviving her. "Quick!" she shouts into the hallway as she places the lifeless body of Mrs. Moores onto the cold white floor. "Get a doctor. We have a code in here!" she continues to scream as she begins life saving CPR after alerting the others with an emergency button. "Breathe, Mrs. Moores, breathe!" she orders as she finishes rescue breaths to begin chest compressions. "Dammit!" she yells frustrated with what appears to be a suicide under her watch. "Mrs. Moores, come on back. I need you to come back!"

She continues yelling as the crash cart is wheeled inside the room, and they immediately begin to shock her chest with the defibrillator, and not soon after, a doctor appears inside, noticing the sheet that is still twisted like a rope hanging off of the bed.

"Suicide…" the female physician whispers as she checks for a pulse before there's another shock with the defibrillator. "How long has she been out?"

"I don't know…"

"When was the last nurse…"

"I was just in here thirty minutes ago, and she was sleeping like a baby. She was asleep, doctor. Check my sheet. She's not on suicide watch…"

"Let's get her hooked up…" she pauses, frustrated with the whole situation. "Now! Let's get her breathing now!"

As they all work to bring Mrs. Moores back to life, more medical personnel pour into the room as they lift Mrs.

Moores onto the bed and roll her down to intensive care, all the while treating her, in hopes that she isn't gone for good.

**

"I'm not going in through the Trails."

"What?" he replies already having had enough.

"I'm not going inside that way. I have to go in through my own neighborhood, Javis. I'll park my car on the side of the road, and we'll walk."

"The side of the road, Alexis?"

"Yeah. The neighbors that live at the corner are on vacation. They're always on vacation now that their children are grown and in college. I can park there, in between their house and the road," she pauses, finally understanding why Javis is so confused. Therefore, she explains, "So my parents won't see my car, Javis. That's all. If they see my car..."

"Oh, oh, yeah, I got you." He wipes his forehead and turns away from the main entrance of Gabriel's Trails in order to head to Alexis' neighborhood. "My mind is all fogged up right now. I don't know what I'm gonna do if they hurt my brother any further. He's all I got left."

"They won't."

"Do you have a gun?"

"No."

Javis takes a deep breath, in disbelief of how tragedies continue to unfold every single time Alexis is around him. The hardcore truth pounds at his skull as he turns into Dominion Lakes and parks in between the house, which is lined with tall, privacy bushes to shield itself from the busy street. He glances at Alexis once more before turning the car off, and then he exits to face the direction he must go to rescue his brother while empty handed. Finally, he hears the passenger's door slam and Alexis approach. His voice stops her in her tracks.

"You don't need to come all the way inside the trails with me. I'll find my way. If I'm not out or you hear gunshots, leave. Go pay my mother's way," he requests, thinking of every possible scenario that he can take care of everyone at the same time, whether he is alive or not. "Will you do that for me...please?"

"Javis. Don't put yourself in this danger for me." After she speaks, he turns back to look at her puzzled, but then finally remembers that she doesn't know that he was involved in deadly events that make him just as much a target without her. He never told her his whole truth. Instead of interrupting her to reveal it, he allows her to finish what she has to say. "I'm the one who killed Bain. I know the guy who sent the text wants you to come, but I'm not stupid. He is using you as bait to get me there. Javis, you know and I know that this isn't gonna stop until I die. Whoever I'm connected to is always in danger until I'm wiped off the face of this earth," she states with a heavy, fearful tremble that is overflowing with pain and guilt. "I don't want anyone to be killed anymore." As she looks at him, it's like she is looking directly at his mother.

During the drive to the trails, she remained mostly quiet after telling Javis exactly where she left Bain's dead body, choking back what she considers the worst horror she'd just done for her own gain – murdering his mother. She realized just how selfish she is, but she also realized that she doesn't know how else to be or survive. Every other way leaves her vulnerable, and that's not the life she's ever lived. Everything in her life has always been a roadmap with no stop signs, however, as time passes, especially since taking the life of Mrs. Moores, she doesn't want to run anymore. What she considers karma has come, and it's guiding her back to the same place where she lost her first love. She doesn't want it to be the place where she loses her second.

"I thought about it on the way up. I'm not afraid anymore, and I don't want to lose you. I'll get your brother set free, and you can go. I deserve to die if it comes down to it," she cries silently as she backs away from Javis slowly.

As tempting as it is for Javis to take her up on her offer, he knows very well what he has also done from within the secrets of the trails. Walking closer to her, he takes hold of her hand quickly, before she backs away any further. "I have blood all over my hands as well. The only other two people who know about it are already dead, along with the people who burned my brother up."

Alexis stares at him stunned and confused. Pulling away from his hand, she asks, "What do you mean?"

"It was me and my brother who killed a guy on the trails. So it's not just you they want anymore. At first they were just gunning for you, but now…"

"They want both of us," she finishes his sentence.

"The other thing is, that's *my* brother, not yours. If he wants you, he'll have to find you himself because what he wants me for, it's a totally different reason. I know it."

"Who did you kill?"

He turns and walks away, refusing to give her an answer because, to him, it's safer that way. He still doesn't trust her, and if he makes it back alive, the secret still needs to be kept. Even more, he needs her safe so that his mom's bill can be paid regardless, which was his main objective from the start.

"Javis," she calls, but he continues walking. "I'll be here. I will." Then, finally as she watches him walk away for possibly the last time, she urges him in a whisper, "Just trust me. Everything I've done, I've done for us." After her words, she looks around in the dark of night until she makes another decision that she knows needs to be made right away before she loses another love in the exact same place. Therefore, she walks back to her car door and gives it a hard slam, loud enough for Javis to hear it. When he doesn't turn around, she runs away from the car to another destination.

**

"Alexis! Alexis, baby, come on down here for a second. I brought something home that you might like. Picked it up from downtown earlier today. Come here, quickly," her mom calls from the foyer as she steps inside the house, tossing her purse and silk scarf onto a small side table. She's been awaiting her daughter's return to the house, having not seen her since she left the night she was questioned by the authorities. "Alexis," she shouts once again but notices a strange silence, so she begins to search for her husband and daughter at the same time, hoping to bring Alexis back to good spirits by bringing her favorite snacks since she was a small girl which she hadn't eaten in years.

In her search, she stops in the kitchen to make a glass of water, and after still not hearing anything, she checks the garage to find that Alexis' car is gone. Immediately, she places the glass of water down onto the counter and rushes to find her husband. "Michael, Michael! Dammit, where is Alexis? Alexis!" She runs up the staircase and into the master bedroom, but still, there is no trace of her husband. "Something's the matter," she whispers to herself as she knows that due to the circumstances, Michael isn't going in to work tonight.

She rushes back downstairs to check every area of the house until she finally walks into the entertainment room. It is there where she discovers her husband sitting alone on the theater seat looking into the darkness of the large flat screen television that hangs from the wall. Already frightened by the fact that he never answered her when she came into the front door, she stalls, unsure of what is going on with him now.

"Michael?" Even though she calls him, he doesn't move a muscle. Glancing around herself, she becomes highly uncomfortable but proceeds to move forward slowly. "Michael, why didn't you answer me when I came inside? Alexis isn't home," she stammers, but he doesn't say a word. "Have you heard from her?"

Instead of answering, Michael only sits there, staring forward as if he doesn't hear a word she's saying. Therefore, she walks forward, taking a deep breath, and when she is standing directly behind him, she raises her hand, placing it on his left shoulder as softly and carefully as she would touch a newborn baby. "Michael?"

"She's not coming back!" he shouts, jumping from the chair with his fists tight and bloodshot eyes that target his wife like she's an enemy.

Stunned and afraid, Mrs. Balentine stumbles backwards in confusion and fear. Noticing his fists and how he glares at her, she feels threatened until he begins to speak once more. He rubs his hand roughly through his hair and as he groans, out of nowhere punches the cushion of the chair like it's a man. At that point, she knows that whatever he's upset with Alexis must be more terrible than she realizes.

"What? What do you mean she's not coming back? She lives here…what, what has happened? She was fine…she just needs to learn to pick up her damn phone!" she worries, already losing her feel on reality as she starts to imagine why her daughter would go missing.

"Lorah, shut the hell up! Would you just shut up for one second? Huh?"

"Fuck you, Michael. I come home with a treat for my daughter because of what just happened, to settle her nerves, and you're telling me to shut the hell up because she never returned home…even after she confessed to being attacked? No, Michael, fuck you," she stresses, pointing directly in his face. "Our daughter has been through enough."

"Oh, Lorah, you're so damn…"

"Damn, what?"

"I talked to her. There! I spoke to *your* daughter, and she rudely gave me her ass to kiss for no apparent reason, Lorah." He storms toward her and takes her by the hands. She pulls back but isn't strong enough to escape his grasp. "All that I've done for her. She just left. Just like that. Said she wasn't coming back. She needs space. Told me she took the money from the safe."

"What?" Lorah responds in shock and disbelief. She finally rips her hands away from her husband. "I'm going to find *our* child, and you should be, too! Sitting here twiddling your thumbs and crying about how she told you to kiss her ass. Well, get up off your ass! This is our child," she screams, removing herself from his presence to walk back toward the front door and retrieve her purse. "I know she's basically an adult now, but this is just ignorant. I'm going to find her...instead of sitting my ass down like you, waiting for more damn trouble."

"Lorah!" he shouts.

"She needs our help!" she screams, slapping the wall. "You help everyone damn else in that hospital, well help her! Help her, dammit! I'm sick of being in denial about this. We are losing her, and I know it. I don't know why or how, but we are. I can feel it."

She stands before him an emotional wreck, not understanding why Michael has been sitting there swelling up in anger against his own daughter who, in her mind, is going through far too much to handle all alone. "I don't care if she's legally grown. She's still a child. She still thinks like a child, Michael."

Dr. Balentine drops his head toward the floor, still fuming at the trap that his own daughter set for him. The betrayal stings, like he's trapped in a huge mound of ants and they are relentlessly attacking him simultaneously. He hears the words that come from his wife's mouth, however, when he goes to counter her again with his vicious words against his own flesh and blood daughter, as he glances back up at Lorah. Directly over her left shoulder and standing on the other side of the staircase is Alexis. She is staring coldly right back at him, having heard every single thing he said.

Quickly, his eyes shift back to his crying wife, snapping from his rage into the only thing left for him to do –

save his own skin. "I'm sorry, Lorah. You're right. Let's go...go find her right now. I'm confused. It's been a long night. Forgive me." He touches her arm, and before she turns around, he pulls her closer and kisses her on the cheek, once more apologizing as he watches Alexis deny her own presence by backing away into the darkness until her parents exit via the front door. Meanwhile, Alexis moves up the staircase after the door slams and enters into her bedroom.

The inside of her closet is long. If standing outside looking in, it appears like a regular sized closet, however, turning left reveals a medium sized passage lined with hanging attire, situated by color. As she walks, the lights shine with her motion as she requested they do for her birthday. At the end of the closet is a full mirror that mimics mirrors that are inside dressing rooms. She lifts the mirror from the hooks, and taped to the backside is a pistol she bought last year from a guy who attended her private school with her. He only appeared straight laced when in fact, he was tainted with crime. No one would ever look his way, and he knew it. Alexis knew it as well. He was her safest bet to get another pistol without getting caught because his straight A's along with the way he assisted in the office and with staff kept him camouflaged. He had always been the one to go to for drugs or weapons, and in her case, she needed a weapon.

As she peels back the masking tape, she recalls the pistol is loaded, therefore, she is careful to not dislodge the bullet. Believing that time is escaping her, she finally pulls the last of the tape from the gun, grasps it inside the palms of both her hands, and backs away from the mirror, allowing it to bang against the wall. At first, her hands quiver, but as she turns to briskly walk back toward the closet door and then her bedroom, she faces the truth. Her hands stop shaking, and she holds the gun with a fierce grip as she watches Bain fall to the ground in her mind. Although she loved him, each time she places herself in that moment, it's not her love that is rekindled, but her wrath. It is that she holds onto as she moves out of her room, then out of the house, and finally on foot to the same trail where the whole war started. She was just too naïve to see it until it was too late.

The grass feels like nails under her shoes, each step relying on the next so the pain of where she is headed doesn't feel so excruciating. When she hits the pavement, her gun is nowhere in sight, having already tucked it in her belt while her shirt covers it. Although she feels like she should hear something from within the trails right now, she doesn't. As she continues walking, however, the hovering sensation of someone watching her becomes overbearing. She immediately stops walking as her chest rises and falls with every breath she takes, but she doesn't turn around. Instead she waits for about ten seconds before fearfully checking behind herself. She sees no one, so she returns to her original direction. The trails are now directly in front of her, but at the sight of them, her mind drifts once again back to a warning that Bain gave her about walking the trail alone beyond a certain point:

"Why did you walk this far up, Lex? You know I don't let you walk this far up the trail…"

"I'm a big girl, babe,"

"Do you see the main road anymore, Lex?"

"No, Bain."

"Nothing but a trail that ends, curving back into where you came from. Nobody can see you anymore, Lex. At that point," he explains, pointing to a boulder that's painted red on the side of the trail, *"Coming in here beyond*

that rock this far up means that you're on your own." He turns her back around so that he can look her in the eyes. "I don't ever want you to be on your own, Lex."

"Javis!" she calls, snapping out of her trance, needing to warn him of not going too far inside. When he doesn't answer, she moves forward, nearing the darkness of the trails until she hears something moving within feet of her. She draws her gun while looking both ways, but because of the street lights that stand at the entrance of each trail, she can't see beyond them. Therefore, she puts her pistol back on her side and walks in, listening for the slightest sound of life from Javis or even his youngest brother Joseph.

~~

He listens intently while stepping slowly, further into the trail, but his concentration is broken when he hears his name being called. Knowing full well that it's Alexis, he turns back to stare into the darkness of the trails, a place he hasn't been in a couple years, and as he continues walking, the shuffle of feet alert him to the fact that he's now standing in the spot where he is most wanted.

"Where the fuck is that girl?"

Javis stands there, his hands stretched out to show that he isn't a threat to anyone there. Still unable to visualize who is speaking to him, he responds, "Where is my brother?"

"Smart ass mouth. You won't have a brother if you think you can ask me questions, young man."

"She's not with me. She called me," he lies. "She told me to come out here, so here I am."

"So if I send some mother fuckers out there to find out who was just calling your damn name..." the voice threatens, knowing full well that Alexis is at the beginning of the trails.

"Okay!" Javis squirms, "Alright, alright. She's here, too. No need to go and..."

"I know she is," he interjects. "Move off the trail. Closer to the trees, and kneel down."

"Which way?" he asks, still unable to locate where the speaker hides.

"Either way," Chief answers before he quietly orders the other two men with him to put away their firearms. "Shit gonna get too loud. One pop, two at the most. You know how shit is on this trail. I got these two guys secure right here with me. Go meet Tryina...don't want her spooked by the weapons. She's on her way."

"You sure, man?"

"Yeah. What the fuck does this look like? This is a fuckin' cipple in my hand right here, and that's his damn, punk ass brother. I got this. Just bring Tryina over here. She should be almost here right now," he states, keeping his eyes on Javis as the two other males walk away inconspicuously through the trees, on the way to find Tryina. Meanwhile, Chief takes a peek down the trail toward the opposite end. He sees no one, but he is aware that Alexis is there which is why he continues to say nothing else except for ordering Javis' hands to the back of his head while holding Joseph by the back of his shirt with a gun pointed directly at his temple.

**

"Hurry up and go," Kaynine states as she steps out of the car. However, when the car remains in position, she looks up from her cell phone. "What are you waiting on? Chief's out there waiting on you. Move!" she continues as she stands on the curb sending a text.

"Who are you texting?" Tryina asks out of paranoia. Kaynine is so calm that it scares her. She may be about to get herself killed for sticking her neck out for Tryina, and it's bothering Tryina's whole mindset knowing that her own death may be tonight as well.

She shuts down her phone, looks Tryina back in the face and responds, "I texted my son, that's who. Tell him I love him. Problems?"

Tryina shakes her head, her hands still sweating from the drive over to the entrance of Dominion Lakes. "No. I'm good. Let me head on over there before…"

"Before you get us both killed?" Kaynine laughs. "That would be a great idea, lil niece. Let me handle this. You just go on over. It won't take long. He doesn't even know I'm here."

"Okay," Tryina states as she rolls up her window, but as she pulls off, she looks back in her rearview mirror. There is Kaynine once again, pulling back out her cell phone, starting to jog toward the trails. The air around her becomes extremely thick inside her vehicle. She feels a panic attack coming on because she doesn't know what to do about the dreadful situation she's found herself in, being that she honestly senses that something isn't quite right. However, she has no choice but to follow the direction of both Chief and Kaynine because they both want and need her in the trails as soon as possible.

Pulling into Gabriel's Trails once again, things seem quieter than usual. Normally, there are people everywhere in the middle of the night. She's used to watching the prostitutes and drug addicts walk in the same areas as the children playing when they should be in the bed asleep. Although things seem out of order, she realizes that they really are in order. The only person out of order is herself. She's never been involved in the day to day criminal life of her brother and his men. That's how she realizes that she may be seeing things differently because now she is involved, and the whole pulse of the neighborhood throbs much more dangerously than ever before, especially since she may be in danger of dying.

"Trust her," Tryina tells herself as she parks her car back at home and begins to hustle her way up to the trails on foot. As she walks, some of the street walkers stare at her and then look away trying not to be noticed. However, Tryina notices them. It's as if they know something in which she has yet to be made aware.

A bead of sweat trickles down her forehead, and she wipes it away as mentally, she repeats to herself to be calm and trust that things will work out. From the corner of her eye, she recognizes one of Chief's goons on his phone. He starts walking back toward the trail as soon as he sees her coming. By the time she reaches the edge of the trail, he is no longer visible. They always find a way to disappear in the darkness. No one knows their spots either because no one dares to search.

Her first footsteps into the trails feel like she's walking on strange land although she's lived here all of her life. She thinks back to seeing her brother walk the streets of

Gabriel's Trails seemingly without a care in the world. He made it look easy, like he had everything under control. No one crossed him, and it was like he was immortal the way people treated him. She feels frail in comparison to him. Even after killing someone, she strips back the pure truth - she's a lightweight and honestly can't handle anything without someone holding her hand and guiding her like a child. As she walks deeper into the trails, her doubts about herself and everyone else draws an insane amount of fear, but she holds on to what street knowledge she has left and decides to play on it and talk a strong game. She is then met by one of Chief's men who lives this life like it's a cake walk while her insides quake. She liked it better when she was never involved.

"What's going down, Tryina?"

She doesn't speak. Instead, she nods.

"Can't speak now?"

"Yes," she says abruptly, promoting a firmer tone with the known killer, "What does Chief want me to see?" He snaps back in an insulting manner.

"How the fuck should I know? You don't need to know until you see it."

"Why the attitude?" she pounces back, knowing full well he's lying about not knowing anything.

He stares at her with a mild form of disgust, and then casts the demeaning nature he has toward her into a smile. "What attitude, baby?" Then, he turns to walk ahead of her. "Come on."

"Where's Chief?"

"Bring your ass…" he states while turning back around to see her, "before I have to drag your ass there myself. I'm just doing my job, baby."

"Let me call him," she says whipping out her phone with her adrenaline pumping, believing that contacting him is the wisest thing to do in her position before following him into the trails. "I need to know he's there," she states, wanting to gain more information about the secretive meeting, thus, buying time just in case.

"Fuck that phone," the man responds already frustrated, reaching back to snatch the cell phone from her hand. His powerful grip is no match for Tryina, and she can only let it go, watching him stuff it inside his pocket which ends up revealing the pistol that's underneath his shirt. Just seeing the pistol forces her to obey and not make any more of a hassle. As he starts walking again, she does as well, noticing that there are even more footsteps coming from behind her. She looks back, but doesn't see a thing nor does she expect to see anything. It's how the trails are now, especially without her brother to ease the tension and fear.

It's not too long down the trail until she sees a figure kneeling down in the darkness. One of the night lights has been broken, obviously on purpose, which causes her to lean forward attempting to see who and what is going on.

"Walk over here," the guy orders.

"Why in the woods?" she retorts, already angry at the way he is speaking to her, but before he answers, another voice answers from the darkness.

"Because he said so and because I told him to bring you."

Tryina recognizes Chief's voice, and without hesitation, she moves beyond the trees and past the man who escorted her. Still not knowing who the guy is kneeling with his head down in silence at the edge of the trails, she ends up terrified when she walks closer to Chief and discovers who else he has at gunpoint.

"Joseph?" Then she whirls around to the other guy who is on his knees at the very edge of the trail, now with a gun pointed at his head by the man who guided her to the spot. "Javis?" Tryina is then confused, turning her attention back to Chief.

"And your girl Alexis is coming, too. It's a gift from me to you and your brother Floss. This time, you won't have to try so hard to kill her. I got your bullets." He pulls out another pistol.

Tryina's heart nearly stops. The first person she thinks about is Kaynine and their active plan to kill Chief. She's wrong. They are both wrong, but she can't say a word about it or the bullets will, without a doubt, in up being for her. As she stands there in the deep of the trails, there's another sound, causing everyone to look in the same direction.

**

"Just who the hell is this I see?" Kaynine whispers as she moves quietly through the trails when she gets an unexpected text message on her cell phone. Keeping her eyes on the thin, light skinned female walking down the trail, she reads the message. "Well oh shit." The message coming in reveals the identity of the female directly in front of her. From there, she pockets her phone after putting it on a light vibrate. Then, she puts down her clutch and removes the pistol. "Little Ms. Alexis. It's gonna be nice to meet you, sweetheart. Who knew I would get such a nice welcome back home?"

She looks both ways, careful to follow a narrow path created long ago that runs parallel to the main trail. Only the gangsters walk this particular line at specific times, and it's right about now that Kaynine is well aware that she may run into one far too soon. With her pistol ready, she feeds off of the moisture that's trapped under the leaves of the trees, and she gains strength from the anticipation of who she is about to encounter. Moving slightly faster than the female she now knows as Alexis, when she turns back to make certain she is still there, she notices that the young woman is suspiciously gone. After checking through the breaks in the trees with no luck locating her again, a broken night light makes her aware that she is in the right spot. "Same old rules of death...break a light" she whispers. "Looks like no one will walk this way tonight who knows better."

As she stands alert and ready to make her move as she waits on Chief to step out into clearer view, she notices the movement of a small light directly ahead of her. From there, she feels the soft vibration of her phone, then it stops. She waits. Then she hears it again, and as she listens, she puts her hand on the trigger. Then, there is one last vibration. She looks up ahead of herself, and there's the cell phone light again moving faster this time and more faint. Kaynine finally turns to face the trail with her gun aiming and ready as she watches another male come up the trail, calling out for Chief, which is music to her ears.

"Hey man, Chief...Chief," he calls, walking confidently toward the area where Chief is located while glancing quickly toward the other side of the trail when he notices a slight bit of motion. "Hold up, Chief, chill for a minute," he says quietly as he pulls out his pistol. Chief already knows who has arrived as he shoves a badly beaten Joseph to the ground prostrate and roughly grabs Javis up to stand beside him to finally become visible on the trail.

"You see her?" Chief asks his criminal counterpart, as he quickly glances back at a trembling Tryina with a grin. While being manhandled by Chief, Javis turns to face his brother again, but Joseph can only muster the strength to continue lying in the dirt, unable to move his legs at all.

"Yeah, I see somebody," the gunman responds, slanting his eyes to the left as he watches the man who has taken over the Trails for years become hungry at the thought of getting revenge for his fallen friends. "But Alexis ain't who the fuck I think it is."

At the words of his friend, Chief becomes severely paranoid, shifting his body and eyes around in the darkness before him, even taking the gun from Javis' head and pointing blindly ahead. Before he utters another sound, however, the metal barrel of the gunman's pistol lands mercilessly at the side of Chief's head. It's not seconds after that a woman steps out from the trees with her pistol aimed directly at the man that runs the streets of Gabriel's Trails.

"Looks like you ran into a bit of a mother fucking problem," she brags, pronouncing every syllable in each word with a grin. "Hey, Chief. Remember me?"

"Kaynine," Tryina calls, but is quickly shut down by her so-called aunt.

"Shut the hell up, Tryina, and stand your ass down." She looks toward the other guy who stands over an obviously incapacitated Joseph awaiting her orders, leaving Chief cornered and within range of a fast death. "Go get her ass. She's up there watching, fucking thinking she's hiding," she orders referring to Alexis.

"Looks like I had my gun pointing at the wrong man, huh?" Chief states, kicking Javis to the side like a non-threatening ragdoll, willing to face the bullets that are aimed his way, and at the same time, planning to point his gun right back at the man who has a gun to his head. "You think I'm gonna let you live, homey?" he questions him, but Kaynine intervenes.

"You ain't crazy, Chief. You're just as sane as my ass except you don't know what the hell being dead feels like. So you pull that damn trigger on my man right there, I'm pulling mine on you...or did you forget my aim is one hundred percent fatal? You know I'm trained for this shit, too. Drop that mother fuckin' weapon," she orders, "because he's not shooting shit tonight."

Smiling, he glances back at the girl he's protected since her brother's death and drops the weapon to the ground. Then, he shakes his head, stopping her from speaking. In the meantime, there Kaynine stands directly in front of him, delighting in his submission. She's overjoyed on the fact that he remembers just how lethal she is as well. "It's been a long damn time since you and your boys tossed me out of here," she continues as Chief voluntarily locks both his hands behind his head, "with damn near nothing to my name. There's just one thing you didn't bet on." She closes in on the man whom used to run just as close to Bain and Floss as she did. "I'd be back."

"You expect me to beg your washed up ass?" he laughs as his train of thought leaves the pistols aimed at him to fall onto the gunman that Kaynine sent off to get Alexis. "Turn your ass around, Kaynine. Your boy came back empty handed, and you better hope when you pull that trigger, I die fast or your ass is next." Then, he turns to the man with the trigger at his head. "Yeah, I'm talking about you, too. Get the fuck outta here, Tryina. Fuck these, clown asses."

"Since we're clowns, laugh, mother fucker," she responds.

At that, Chief lunges at Kaynine like a bulldog at its prey, but he winds up submitting to the firepower that makes its way to the pit of his stomach. As he falls powerless to the filthy ground before everyone, his only focus is on the woman who shot him as she kneels there in awe while he cups his stomach in both palms of his hands, struggling to hold it together. They stare through one another, once old friends and now lethal enemies.

"I should have killed you when I saw you," Chief smiles as he seems to enjoy grasping the death he gave to so many others.

"You think so? Remember," she responds, "I'm the one who had your back when you aimed that gun in a fuckin' rage at Bain while his back was turned to you. Remember that? I saved your life, and look at the thanks you gave me for it. You just let them toss me out...even after you knew the fuckin' truth about what he did to me. So fuck you. Die by the same sword you live by." She stands. "Fuck your stomach. Here's one for the head." Kaynine fires, and Chief catapults backwards at full force by a bullet to the front of his skull in the midst of a terrified whimper from the only other female voice in their circle.

As Kaynine removes herself and her mind from a dying Chief, no one else pays him any loving attention either as one of the guys pat him down. From there, they all focus on the woman with the gun. Kaynine looks over to a sobbing Tryina and waves her over.

"Baby niece, it's for the best. I'm back, and I told you I would handle it."

"I've known Chief for a long time. We were wrong. He protected me, and he wasn't even here to kill…"

"*Kill you*? Ask them. Yes he was. Tell her, fellas," she orders as Tryina stares on in shock at how they obey and even validate her story. "And don't either one of you other mother fuckers move," she calls out to Javis and Joseph. "If you think we won't shoot you, try us."

Unable to watch Chief lie there alone, Tryina falls to her knees directly in front of him and remembers all that he's done for her in the past since her brother left the earth. "Chief, Chief. Were you gonna kill me?" she weeps quietly, feeling a deep loss inside her soul. "It has to be a lie, please tell me…" she cries. "I'm sorry."

As gently as she can, she removes herself from his presence, just as he did from hers, but into another realm. When she stands up, she faces the woman she's respected and loved for so long. "I need to know the whole story, Kaynine. How do you expect me to trust anybody when all of you keep secrets from me?"

"There wasn't a secret kept. He was gonna frame you," a gunman says, glancing at Kaynine. "Just like he framed you at the house. I should know, shouldn't I? Wasn't I there? He was gonna have you kill these two and the one up the road named Alexis. You go to prison and that's that. You should be thanking Kaynine."

"Yeah, Tryina," Kaynine agrees with a bitter heart, but instead of addressing Tryina any further, she finishes up with the two young men who remain stationary in the dirt of the trails who witnessed everything that happened. "Who are these fine, young men?" she asks sarcastically.

"A part of the family that killed Floss."

"No. Not anymore. Derrick is already dead! Joseph is innocent. He's cripple," shouts Tryina as she watches Kaynine lift her pistol. "He's beat up enough," she hollers, knowing that Javis is the only way Joseph will make it in life and refusing to stomach anymore deaths by her hands or anyone else's.

"Yeah, he's the cripple boy who used to live down on the corner, always totin' that Bible and shit. He ain't no harm, just bait. Far as I know, to be honest with you, Kaynine," continues one of the men who is now in full allegiance to her, "they won't talk. They have too much dirt on themselves to talk and the past has proven they won't talk."

"Good because that isn't nor has it ever been my fight. I was just coming to protect my niece...and I kept my word...every single word." Kaynine puts her pistol inside her pants and reaches out to take Tryina by the hand. Then, in the softest tone that Tryina has heard since reuniting with her, Kaynine assures her, "I'll fill you in on everything. We'll fill each other in...away from these guys." She cocks her eyes up at them both and advises them to dispose of Chief where he can be found quickly. Then she whispers, "Find Alexis, and fuck the laws of Gabriel's Trails. Kill her wherever she is for no other reason but that she knows too much. I could give a fuck if she shot Bain honestly. As far as these young men, take them back where they need to be. Get them something to eat. We might need them at another time. It's a new day." Then, she backs away from the man's ear and repeats it out loud. "It's a brand new damn day! Fellas, I'm sorry about all this. They will take you back..."

"No. No...we'll find a way. They might kill us anyway," responds Javis.

"I'll kill you if you don't go," Kaynine responds calmly. "They aren't gonna do shit. Enemy of my enemy is my mother fuckin' friend, friend. Like I said, you'll be safe wherever you need to go. This is our bond, and bonds aren't meant to be broken. Can't you see that?" she asks as she shifts her eyes downward and lightly kicks who is now a dead Chief. "It's nice to meet you, and now, you're free to go." From there, Kaynine and Tryina walk down the trail, retrieve her clutch that she left by a tree, and continue back down the trail until they reach the streets of Gabriel's Trails.

Joseph remains silent as his brother falls down next to him in an attempt to lift him from the ground, totally ignoring the bonding pledge from Kaynine. "Joseph, I'm here. Let me help you up. Can you at least move, man?" When Joseph doesn't respond, he stands up and straddles him to lift him underneath both his arms, but instead of assisting, Joseph forcefully fights against him, causing an already emotionally broken Javis to scold him. "What's wrong with you? It's me, man. Get up! We have to go and go now."

"Move out of the way, youngster," one of the gunmen interjects. "When your brother lifts your ass up, get the fuck up. Either let me see effort or we'll be forced into other plans. This man must think we're 911 or some shit," he jokes to his counterpart. "We don't lift anybody unless we've already killed 'em. Man the hell up." He waves his pistol at Javis as an order to lift his brother again. This time, when Javis goes to pick him up, Joseph reacts with all his strength, nearly standing on his own. It becomes clear to Javis that his brother doesn't want to be anywhere near him, but for the sake of survival, he allows Javis to help him back to the car from which he was kidnapped. They remain silent towards one another all the way back to their destination – the hospital - but they both wonder who the woman really is that rescued them from their deaths by killing the neighborhood's one and only Chief.

**

"Kaynine, we can't just walk back through here like this. Chief is dead, and you shot him. People are gonna see us and…"

"They need to see us. Watch this. Bring your ass and I'm not saying it twice. I'll tell you the story on the way back to your place, so fuck these people. Trust me, they already know more than you do about my ass. There was only two badder than me, and that mother fucker I shot back there thought he was the third. If there's one thing you need to learn from me is this, Tryina, walk with your head held high, and don't let people see your fear, even if you're guilty as hell. I started out here," she continues as she watches Tryina stand taller and take stronger strides to mimic hers as those who are on the streets watch and whisper. "I started out right here, and you already know that me and your brother were basically in love. We were too scared to take it that seriously, but we were. Anyway, one day, your brother came to me in a fury. He'd never been that way with me before…watch your step," she warns Tryina as she makes a near miss of the uncovered pothole.

"They keep coming to fix it…"

"I know. And they keep lifting that shit off again the same night. It's a drug dump. You know that. Drop the innocent act. Your brother taught you that shit, but I know you have some fang in you. I know you better than you know yourself. But uhm…Floss…he came in there raising up at me. I'll never forget that day. I was sitting right over there," she continues, pointing to the home that once belonged to Bain. "I was in there with him while Bain was out doing his thing. He'd left us alone in there. I was smoking a cigarette at the kitchen table when Floss came and turned that table over right there on me. I fell to the floor, banged my head on the wall, and then he kicked me in my legs, telling me to stand up…"

~~

"Stand your ass up!"

"Floss, stop," she begged while struggling to lift herself up on the edge of the toppled table. "Stop kicking me. What the hell is wrong with you? Let me go!" she screamed as Floss yanked her up from the floor himself.

"What's that I hear?"

Kaynine punched his hand off of her shirt, breaking free from his grasp as she became horrified at his wild eyed gaze. "I don't know! Leave me alone!"

"Let me tell you this," he lunged once more, causing Kaynine to leap over the table and crash against the corner of the wall with nowhere left to go. "Bain wouldn't lie to me. He never has, and he never will. You've been walking around me like nothing happened for days, fuckin' smiling in my damn face," Floss continued as tears welled up in his eyes, but he wiped them away before they fell. It was then that she knew that Bain revealed what happened between them, except it was as plain as day that he'd twisted the story.

"Floss, I didn't do anything to you or against you. I didn't tell you anything because I could handle it. He would have killed you, and you know that."

Floss backed up, confused at what Kaynine was saying. He smelled like he'd been drinking, and the way he looked, he'd been up for a while, which was normal, but that time, his behavior was the most abnormal that she'd seen. He had an evil in his eyes that was brand new. Even when he taunted and abused his enemies, he always thought it was funny. It was only this time where his emotions seemed to be too much for him to handle.

"Fuck you talking about, Kay?" With his eyes barely open, he began to stagger around, so she reached for his hand. When he felt her warm touch, he looked down at the soft hands he'd grown to love, caressing his hardened skin, and he rewarded the favor of love with a calm and tender touch to her face as he finally allowed the tears to break from his eyes which was something no one in the Trails had ever witnessed.

Kaynine finally took the lead, lifting both their hands and wiping the tears from his eyes. Hesitant to give full details of that day she was overtaken by the evils of Bain, she stood there with him in silence until he pushed her hand down gently from his face. From there, the momentary softer gaze that he had for her began to disappear, and as fast as the tears came, the internal rage from his body dried them all up, causing Kaynine to explain even further.

"Floss, you were asleep. He called me over, and I thought things were going to be okay, you know?" she spoke with a lightened tone. "But things ended up not so okay, Floss, and it wasn't me. Believe me! He told me to undress...and I did. I had no choice. I was scared. I had to do it...I didn't know what else to do, Floss. That's Bain..."

"*That's Bain?*" he questioned, taking what she said as a put down to him and his worth in comparison to the man he sees as a blood brother. "And just who the fuck do you think I am, Kay? Who?" he shouted.

"Floss. You're Floss. I know who you are, and I love everything about you," she whispered while backing away. "Floss, you know me," she cries. "This doesn't change anything, especially the way I feel about you. I didn't want him to hurt you…"

He didn't wait for her to finish. "Now get the fuck outta this place."

Kaynine failed to understand exactly what he meant by his words. Loyalty was everything to him, and him ordering her to leave the place could mean only one thing. His eyes never blinked nor did they wavier from staring straight through to her soul. "What…are you kicking me out of the house? Are you going to at least talk to me about it…I know that's your boy, but he's lying," she pleaded, but it fell on deaf ears.

"Bain wouldn't lie to me…like a whore would. Like you said, I was asleep. You could have called me. You didn't fight. I don't believe none of that shit you're saying. I would have killed him myself and took the blow back. Now get your ass out of these Trails, or I'll kill you myself. But make sure you remember *this* name. I'm mother fuckin' Floss, and I got no love for your ass anymore. Don't you forget that shit."

Kaynine couldn't move, in disbelief at her banishment from Gabriel's Trails, but when he pulled his pistol, there was no choice.

~~

"And that's when I had to leave, Tryina. It was just like that," she finishes her story as they arrive at Tryina's home, and she opens her front door. As they go inside, everything seems different, just as different as the walk back to her place felt. Everyone who was on the streets looked, but no one questioned or approached her and Kaynine in the dead of night. The prostitutes moved from her path, and some of the children who were still lingering around their front doors, were taken by their mothers as Kaynine was spotted on the block. Lights were turned off and some came on as they passed by, and it was the gangsters, both hidden and visible, who stood firm, in allegiance as if they already knew and respected the woman who killed Chief. Through all the onlookers, Kaynine never flinched.

"I didn't know anything about that, Kaynine. I apologize…for my brother. He didn't know, and he never said anything to me about it," she responds as she tosses her keys to the chair, but is stopped when Kaynine connects with her wrist.

"Now you have to do one more thing to take the heat off of us," she says as she double checks the locks on the door, her confident demeanor suddenly changing to one of worry and angst. "The reason we didn't die on the way back is that I arranged a payoff for your life."

"You did what?" Tryina asks, quickly starting to panic as a result of Kaynine act out of character.

"Show me where the money is," she responds, flaring her hands around as if there is no time. "If you look back outside that door, if I walk back out there with no money signal, they will heat us both up," Kaynine stresses, pulling her ponytail into a full bun on the top of her head and moving to the blinds to see outside. "These mother fuckers will kill us, now do what I say! Have I been wrong yet? You heard them back at the trails. Chief was setting you up, so I had to take him out, now you owe me. Keep us alive," she pleads pointing to her chest and then pushing her finger dead center into Tryina's. There's no rush from Tryina, however, as she becomes frozen in fear, resulting in Kaynine shaking her viciously by her shoulders. "Wake the hell up! This is how the streets are run, T. Just like this. Nothing is free. That walk down the Trails we just did, that wasn't even free. Chief's death wasn't free. I promised them. I still have connections, but we both need that money…not all of it, but enough to take the heat off."

"Is that who you were texting?"

Kaynine releases her and stands tall, unshaken although she'd been caught in a falsehood. "Yeah, that was who I was really texting. No…it wasn't my son. I lied for your sake. What you don't know, you don't need to know. That's the law of the Trails. You know that."

"At that point, you didn't have to lie, though?"

"Do you wanna die, baby girl?" she interrupts, tired of the back and forth. "Because we will if you stand around here like you're damn five years old asking questions. Ask that shit later. Where is the money?" Tryina doesn't move. Kaynine then walks to the window and beckons Tryina forward. "Look. Look your ass out there. Now, I have one gun. They have plenty," she stresses, gritting her teeth while convincing Tryina of the obvious. "I'll take my grave, but can you?"

Without another word, Tryina walks slowly to the back room. As she walks, she asks, "How much money are we talking about?"

"Listen, Tryina, it's not to give away. It's to keep rule. Without rule, these brothers go hungry. Sure, we're paying them, but afterwards, you own this. They need proof or they take it, and the kingdom falls. They know me. Unlike your brother, they know what went down, and how I was cast out from someone else's lies. I'm a woman of my word."

At that, Tryina pushed the bed over in the bedroom and taps the floor with her shoe. "This isn't all. There's a map in the wall. Most of it is buried in the trails, some out back, but it's all plastered in this wall. I never needed to go into the wall…ever. See that small pen mark…all it takes is knocking it out. A hammer. That's the roadmap, but here where I'm standing is where the rest is. Just lift it up. See. This is what I use to take care of myself."

"Well, let's get some of it out, and show it to them so life can go on then," Kaynine says with a smile. "It's gonna finally be alright. One day, you can get out of this life, but slowly." At that Kaynine stands back and watches as Tryina lifts the floor board to uncover stacks of cash. Just the smell of it causes her to lift her pistol, and when Tryina turns to show her the money, she finds herself staring down the barrel of a gun. All the money in her hands falls, and fear throws her back, causing her to bang her head on the side of the bed's headboard. She weeps at the sight of the only woman in the world she trusts holding a gun to her forehead. Tears flow heavily, but Kaynine doesn't care at all as she begins to speak.

"Little Tryina. When I left my house, I'd already found out my plan didn't go through. Fucking trying to get around Chief is like a damn maze, but…"

"Don't kill me, Kay, please," she cries, but Kaynine keeps talking.

"Macy…your dead friend. I knew her. I hired her sloppy ass. Her dumb ass was supposed to do the job and get her ass paid, not Tony. Do you really think I can *smell death*, dumb ass? Who the fuck can do that shit unless there is a rotten damn body? I was told you shot him, " she states as she watches the horror bind Tryina's mind. "Your problem is that we always shielded your ass from every damn thing that you can't spot bullshit when it's right in your face. I was happy to come and finish this shit up because truth is, that's *my son's money*." Bitterness and brokenness boil themselves in the solution of rage that has built in Kaynine for years as Tryina stares into the eyes of the only person more deceiving than Satan himself.

"Kaynine!" Tryina cries loudly continuously, in efforts to make someone outside rescue her. She yearns for her brother and Chief, the two men who continuously taught her to trust no one, and she begins to mourn the fact that she hasn't listened. "Please! I'll give you the money! I don't know your son, and I don't even know how you think it's his, but take it. All of it! I'll leave."

"I had to carry that baby for nine damn months on the fuckin' streets because of your brother and Bain. I failed to tell them one damn thing. When I delivered my baby, it was also Bain's delivery. Now, take a wild guess who took me in and hired me to get all my baby's money back, sweetheart?" Before Tryina asks who, she answers, "Bain's mother." One second later, the gun fires, and Tryina is left with a bullet lodged in her head. No one comes to her aid. Kaynine backs away and wipes a lone tear from her eye. "You're not quite the next in line. Sleep tight."

She slowly walks out of the bedroom and back down the hall, memories of everything she's been through up to this point in her life, memories which include caring for Tryina when she was younger. Her tough exterior breaks, and before she reaches for the door knob of the front door, she cradles her stomach and moves to the floor, struggling to destroy the pain she feels inside. She hears the footsteps on the porch, but she doesn't open the door. Instead, she lays her back against it, sobbing until she can sob no more. When she gains control of herself again, she stands up tall, wipes her face, reaches for the sunglasses that are in her clutch, and although it's the dead of night outside, she puts them on. From there, she opens the front door. More gunmen push past her as she stands there emotionless in order to clean up the mess. As another gunman stands at the bottom of the small porch taking mental notes of what homes to hit if word gets out, she finally speaks.

"Go get my son and his grandmother."

Meanwhile, back at Dominion Lakes, Alexis cowers at the back of the house, sitting underneath her huge deck trembling after hearing the gunshots, believing that Javis is now dead.

DECEPTION

AT

GABRIEL'S

TRAILS

V

DECEPTION AT GABRIEL'S TRAILS V

Some will come to Gabriel's Trails to gain power, and some will come to meet their deaths.

In this finale of Deception at Gabriel's Trails, the taste of revenge is at hand, and each player craves the death of a specific woman or man. In this struggle for power, something is always at stake. You must be willing to pull the trigger or be willing to meet your own questionable fate.

In Gabriel's Trails, life is a brutal game of chess. It's all about who can lay the kings and queens to rest...and take over.

"Come on, Joseph. Get out of the car, man," Javis prompts him in a low tone while never moving his eyes from the gunmen who brought them back to the hospital. Due to the fact that his mother is admitted, he is careful not to breathe a word about it to the henchmen who are patiently waiting for Joseph to get out of the car.

"Remember what we told you. Your brother got jumped by a mob of guys on the way home from school. You got that? If word gets out that it happened in Gabriel's Trails or by any one of us, dig your graves."

"Yeah, I got it. Just going to get him checked out is all. Come on, Joseph."

"I can stand on my own," replies a defiant Joseph.

At his words, the henchmen laugh and start to move the car slowly forward as Joseph attempts to get a firm grip on himself to move away from the vehicle. "How about now? How about you hold on to the car by holding on to the hood? Will that work?"

"No," Javis answered sharply. "My brother can walk just fine. I got him. Joseph," he states once more, this time, not in the mood to watch his brother's griping or complaining. "Let's go. We need to get inside…now." From there, he grabs his brother at the arm and tosses it around his shoulders. That's when the gunmen speed off, not waiting another second for anymore conversation or to ensure the two beat-up, young men make it inside.

"This is all your fault."

"I don't have time to listen to you blame me."

"Who else then? You and that girl…again!" he shouts. "Isn't it enough she caused all this on us, and now you run around with her more? Look at me, man. Look! Everybody is getting killed or hurt except for you and her. I wonder why?" he questions the situation due to his growing distrust of his brother.

Javis cringes at his words and restrains himself from dropping his own brother down in the streets. Instead, he continues walking toward the hospital's entrance remaining silent. His brother's breath beats his skin, reminding him of the lives that were taken in his family and how precious Joseph's life is to him despite his brother's harsh words. It is this that keeps Javis' temper from flaring quiet and focused on taking care of not only Joseph, but getting his own mother the physical and mental health she needs, regardless of the ideas his brother has about him.

"You don't know anything. As a matter of fact, you just stay up there with mom. Hold your head down when we walk in. She should be asleep by now, and when she wakes up, just tell her…" he pauses, in thought about what to say next. "We don't have the money to pay for a couple of bruises that will heal on their own. I'll get some ice from the nurse's station. We won't say you got jumped. We are going to say you fell on concrete steps at the park. It leaves the situation closed, not open to the cops and a full out investigation."

"I bet you don't want an investigation," he replies sarcastically.

"Man, what are you trying to say? Just say it," he strains, staring his brother in the face in awe of what continues to come from his lips.

"You're doing this. It all makes sense now. Just like they said in the car. It's you and her. It's gotta be."

"Me and her? Is that what you think? Really? I'm getting my own family hurt on purpose? I went back to that girl for one thing and one thing only, and that's her money. She's in love with me as sick as that sounds, but she chased me down on the streets. You don't know what the hell you're talking about. She has the money, and she has even more where that came from. We just have to stay alive until I can get it." He starts to walk once again. "Mom's bills are basically already paid, and if I can get more, we can leave…again."

"So you don't care at all for her?"

Javis ignores his question, but Joseph pulls away, able to hold himself up, no longer willing to constantly accept help from anyone because from the looks of things, he may be closer to being on his own than what he once thought.

"I asked you a question."

"Come on, Joseph. You're gonna fall, and…"

"Answer me!" he shouts, his voice growing so loud and deep that those who walk the sidewalk stop to see if everything is under control. Javis lifts his hands in the air with a smile, signaling that everything is peaceful, no matter the sound, and turns to Joseph.

"She's all I have to talk to, man. I don't love her. If I did, I wouldn't be taking what she has." Javis' voice and demeanor then lowers, holding his head down in shame as his brother looks on speechless. "But to be honest with you, when she chased me down the other day, I saw you at the screen door when I got home. No, I didn't tell you anything, but it's been hard, bro. You don't know. You never did know. I held her at gunpoint. That's where we got the money from the last time. As far as investigations are concerned, there's no way I can call the cops because with one word from multiple ways, I could go away for crimes that I just had to do, not wanted to do. I had to do, man. All that crap you see with me with her…that's a mask. If I can keep her happy, I can keep us happy until we can break apart and go our separate ways again. I understand her, though. I understand her in ways that others just don't. I can even tell you, man, that she even saved my life," he continues, recalling the events where if she didn't intervene, he would be in prison or even dead.

Joseph thinks back to what Chief told him in the car on the way to the Trails. It all makes perfect sense to him now, however, he can't shake the anger he has for Alexis, not like his brother can. Instead of talking about it anymore, he limps ahead of his brother, and when Javis tries to assist him, he calmly refuses.

"I got it. I'm almost a man of my own now. I have to stand on my own two feet, even if they are wobbly. Let's just get inside. You don't have to get any ice for me or make an excuse for me. Now that I know what's going on, I can handle it."

Javis stands there for a second and watches the boy whom he has always thought of as a baby brother, behave so much more like a young man than he's ever taken notice of before. As Joseph limps to cross the street directly in front of the sliding doors, Javis rushes to his aid but stops just short of grabbing him at his arm. Instead, he watches as he does it all on his own, and it is only then that he realizes he no longer needs to care for and protect him like a son, but as a brother.

As the sliding doors close behind Joseph, Javis follows behind him inside. For the first time since Joseph's kidnapping, after the elevator doors close before them, they embrace tightly and don't release each other until they reach their mother's floor. The elevator door opens to the sound of a ring, and they both exit, this time once again, leaning on one another as they walk through the double doors toward the nurses' station for some ice.

"Excuse me, nurse. I took a really bad tumble earlier as I was on my way back here. I need some ice. Would I be able to get some from you?"

"Sure...sure," the nurse answers with a confused yet concerned appearance as she moves to get the ice, but instead brings back an ice pack. "Aren't you the young men from...Mrs. Moores' children?"

"Yes," Javis answers. "We're here so late because..."

The nurse waves her hand and rushes around the counter to stand directly in front of them. I'll direct you to another room. Your mother has been moved. Will you follow me, please?"

"Wait a minute, wait a sec," Javis asks, noticing the nurse's urgent expression. "Why was she moved? Is she okay?"

"Mister..."

"Javis...and this is my brother Joseph," he interrupts, growing impatient at the nurse for stalling.

"Please, I will have the liaison escort you down to ICU, and from there..."

"ICU?" Joseph interjects. "There was nothing wrong with my mom this morning when I left. Nothing! What do you mean? Did she have a heart attack?"

"Joseph, calm down. Just," Javis continues, placing both his hands atop his head trying not to have a breakdown. "Just take us there. I need to see my mom. That's all."

"Come with me. Please, just come with me. I will escort you down myself." The nurse continues to walk as they follow her to the elevator. Instead of speaking, they are patient as the elevator takes them on a ride down to the fourth floor. As they exit, the nurse escorts them to a side door and asks them to wait there as she gets a key. "Unfortunately, I have to gain clearance for you because there are only specific times that visitors or family members can go back. I will have someone from this floor with more details about the matter concerning your mother come speak with you as soon as I return in just one minute."

The time that lapses between them and the answers about their mother seems like days when it's only been just one full minute or two. There are people sitting in the waiting area which is adjacent to the door where they stand, and when another nurse comes through the doors, the only attitude that the young men have toward her is one of expectation. As she unlocks the door, a female doctor comes behind, entering the room along with them.

"I'm Dr. Baker, young men, and you are?"

"We're Mrs. Moores' sons, Javis and Joseph."

Before the doctor continues, she notices Joseph's bruising and orders the nurse to get a couple bandages. "Don't worry yourself about the charges. I hear you fell down pretty hard," she states, having already noticed his disability. "So the nurse will tend to it appropriately. There is absolutely no easy way to tell you this," she pauses, aware of the gravity of the situation, "but your mother has died.

She passed away roughly two hours ago by asphyxiation due to suicide."

The silence after her words is far too loud. It's so loud that Javis doesn't sit to hear anymore. Joseph drops from the chair and onto the floor, directly in front of Dr. Baker's feet. When she tries to help him up, the familiar wail of death that the doctor has grown accustomed to hearing but never accustomed to ignoring, breaks her heart into pieces. Tears break through the stone face she fights to keep, and she ends up cradling the beat up young man in her arms as he wails all alone while his brother storms through the halls of the hospital.

"Mama! Mom!" Javis' voice rumbles against the walls as he pounds his fists against the stubborn double doors that won't budge. Those who are inside the waiting area, some asleep on chairs and others wide awake, are startled by the noise, but they don't move as many of them have learned very well the sound of agony and pain when a loved one dies. The pounding on the door continues, now with Javis' feet joining his fists, but before he starts in another round of desperation, male nurses and security come and open the double doors. Javis bolts into them like a football player on the field against his opponents, but he is subdued as they pin him to the wall, vigorously attempting to restrain him as he quickly finds out that his mother is being moved to a larger room to make space for more family.

"Please, please, son," the security guard begs, struggling to hold a distraught Javis at peace. "I understand. Trust me I do, but you have to help us here as we try to help you. You're a strong young man, now just please."

"I want to see my mother! Mama!" Veins protrude from his forehead all the way down to through his fists as the disbelief he feels attacks the pain that begins to pound his chest. "Get off of me! Let me go…" he continues as he begins to slide down the wall. "Just let me go. Mama…" His head rocks back and forth against the smooth, cold wall as his eyes seal shut. His own breath feels like his worst enemy as he doesn't want to fill his own lungs up with air anymore.

The security guard and nurses slowly remove their firm grip on him, and as he sits there, he notices the direction in which the nurses are looking. It's the room where his mother lies, and just like a track star at the hurdles, he jumps up and races toward the room. Before they can place another hand on him, he is already at his mother's side as she lies underneath the bleached white sheets that are pulled all the way up to her neck. Her hands have already grown cold, but her face appears as lovely as it ever has in life.

"Mama," Javis cries. "I found him, mama. I found Joseph. He's here, he's right in there. You could have waited on me. I told you that I would never let you down. I would always take care of you, no matter what I had to do. Joseph!" he shouts through the closed door, and it's not more than one minute that Joseph is being assisted into the room by the same nurses that held him back.

"See, Mama, look," Javis gets up from her side and walks over to Joseph, removing him from the nurses' arms as if revealing her youngest son to her would bring her back from the dead. "Look. Here he is. He took a bad fall. That's why he was late. Mama," he calls, waiting on her to answer as Joseph falls onto the base of the bed in complete agony, having no words that can spell out his loss and pain. "Mama!" he shouts once more before placing his head atop her chest and weeping profusely. "Don't leave us. Please…" There is no such thing as comfort in this moment of gloom, and after minutes of weeping on his mother's chest, he raises his head in anger. Then, he looks toward the door, storms over, and pulls back the large, heavy curtain that allows him to stare directly into the eyes of security. Joseph never looks up as he cradles his mother's hand like it's the only thing that matters to him in life. Javis, then, walks outside to stand directly in front of the nurse's station.

"My mother...who killed her?" As he speaks those words, the security guard moves toward him, believing that he is about to act irrationally. Javis notices his movement from the corner of his eyes, but that doesn't stop him from asking again in a way that is completely out of character for a young man as respectable as he has always been. "I just asked a question. Who the fuck killed my mother?"

"Young man..."

"She didn't kill herself," he replies, wild-eyed and ready to attack. "Who was on duty and who was in her room?" That's when he stops talking and glances down at the counter as if he's watching images move around atop of it.

"Young man, are you okay?" the nurse asks, moving around the counter slowly as she watches Javis raise his head once again slowly, like he's in a daze. Then, he backs away from the counter with his hands spreading out to his sides as if he is warning anyone not to come near him. "Did anyone see a girl up there?"

"Up where, son?"

"Dammit, I'm not your son! Did anyone tell you they saw somebody in my mother's room upstairs?" When they only stare back at Javis like he needs some medication, it infuriates him. "Answer me!" His voice is powerful enough to be taken as a threat, but before security touches him, he turns to view his mother, and decides. "It must have been her." Then he bolts from the hospital, leaving his brother and his heart behind. As he enters his mother's car, his rage overflows as he hones in on the one person whom death always tends to follow. "It had to be her. My mom would never kill herself."

**

Unlocking the back door after moving from underneath her deck, Alexis drops to the floor and continues to crawl inside her massive home. The size of the house only adds to her loneliness as she recognizes that she has absolutely no one now that she is certain, in her own mind, that Javis is dead and gone. The tears haven't stopped as she recalls the request he made of her to take care of his mother which will never happen. His mother is dead, and she died by her hands.

"I'm so sorry, Javis," she moans as she curls up onto the cold floor. "Please, come back, please. We were supposed to be together. I was coming, I was…but I got scared. I got scared," she continues, trembling while staring straight ahead, hating her life just as much as she loves it. She puts her gun on the floor, and moves toward the drawer full of china that her mom cherished since her wedding. It is there where she finds the knives, still covered in a thin, plastic wrap. Pulling the plastic down from the knife starts the emotional release that Alexis so desperately needs, and as she finally holds the bare knife by the handle, she presses it against the inside of her wrist, slowly dragging it across her skin until it finally breaks. The warmth of blood eases her pain and sets her mind at ease as she continues to deepen the gash until she pauses and opens her eyes to a sound coming from the back of the house.

Quickly, she stands and shoves the bloody knife back into the drawer, believing that it's her parents returning home, but as she rushes to escape being seen, she notices a larger, more threatening shadow at the glass door that doesn't match the stature of her parents. She also remembers that she left the door open and that her gun is on the floor.

She runs back to retrieve the gun from the floor as the shadows fiddle around at the door. Then, she bolts inside her home, frantic, assuming the only thing left that makes sense - her enemies of Gabriel's Trails have finally broken their rule of law. They've decided to seek her beyond the protection of their own neighborhood in order to intrude on her wealthy stomping grounds just to find and murder her.

Blood drips from her wrist as she runs up the staircase, contemplating turning back to exit the front door, but unsure of whether someone else is outside blocking her escape from that direction. Her car is still parked at the far end of the street, and the only way she can move is by foot. She lifts her arm to force the blood flow in reverse as it leaves a trail to her location. As she stands in front of her bedroom door, fear consumes her as she hears the door shut followed by footsteps. From there, she returns to the furthest place of protection that she knows to wait – the back of her bedroom closet. The barrel of the gun aims toward the entrance with her finger on the trigger.

~~

"Where are we going, grandma? I'm tired. I don't feel like going anywhere right now," the boy complains as his grandmother shuts the blinds.

"We're going somewhere you've never been before. Get your stuff together, and come on. Put on something nice other than those pajamas. I have another outfit laid out for you right there, already on the bed. See," she responds. Her hair is pulled back into a braided bun at the very back of her head, and her makeup is flawless, hiding what she considers the barely visible lines near her eyes that have crept up since she lost the most important people in her life. Although Jeneeva has aged slightly since the death of her son, she is still the most elegant woman to have ever walked the streets of her old neighborhood. "I need you to hurry up. I have somewhere to take you. Your mother's already there. Don't let me come back in here and get you, sweetheart," she states in a loving tone, never having had to raise her voice to anyone for as long as she can remember. "You have about two minutes."

"Yes, ma'am. Brush my teeth, too?"

"No, just come on. You'll be going back to sleep when we get there."

As she walks out of the room, she heads to a locked drawer which connects to her bed. Atop her dresser underneath her jewelry box is a key. After she grabs it, she kneels down at the bed and slides her hand across the bottom of the rail until she hits a piece of tape that holds another key. She yanks it down and proceeds to open the drawer which has a double lock.

Inside the drawer is loads of cash, stacks of hundreds, but she shoves that aside. Instead, she reaches for what is beneath all the money, something that she considers as an automatic pass for any and everything in her old neighborhood. It's Johnny Bain's gun, her deceased husband. There's an inscription on the side with his name on it. It's the same gun he used to execute a man in broad daylight while all eyes were on him. Everyone saw the inscription in red, big bold letters, but no one dared utter a word. There was no mistake who shot the man dead on the streets, and it was her husband that almost begged anyone to utter a word or call the law. The man lay there on the street dead for twelve hours until the sun went down as her husband sat atop his car and guarded the body he'd slain, all the while allowing his pistol to dangle from his finger exposing who runs the streets.

"Grandma, I'm done. Can I go lay down on the couch until you come out?"

"Yeah, baby. Go ahead. I'm on my way out now."

He doesn't respond, but instead, runs to jump on the living room couch. There are huge pillows atop the couch, and every time he visits his grandmother, his favorite is the one with the gold stripe the runs clear down the middle of the black. It's his favorite because the golden stripe is soft and smooth like velvet, and he loves to place is cheek directly on it.

Located directly in front of him on the center table is a picture of a man whom he has never met. The photo sits inside a brown frame, and on the lap of the man whom he's never met is a boy who looks just like him. He's asked his grandmother who it is before, many times, and the answer she gives him is *"That's my son with his daddy."* When he asks where they are, she only says one thing, *"Gone."*

"Are you ready, baby? Come on,' his grandmother states as she exits the hallway to find him gazing at the framed picture on the table again. "And bring that, too."

"You mean, you want this picture?"

"Yeah, that one," she responds with a smile. "You can keep that one. I have a spare."

"So this is my grandpa and your son, right? How come they don't ever come back from being gone?"

"Sometimes, people don't come back. That's why you've always got to be prepared for them to leave." She kisses his cheek and they both walk out of the house while Kaynine's son follows behind confused as to why they are getting in the back seat of a random car. He doesn't ask questions, however, as he is too excited to be given his first picture of his grandfather and who he assumes is his uncle. It's not long before they enter into a place where he's never been but where his grandmother's heart never left.

As the driver moves them from block to block inside Gabriel's Trails, Jeneeva purposely turns her head away from the location where she lost her husband forever. That day was so hard for her that it caused her to remain sheltered for months to years until the one day her son decided that he could handle things for the both of them. With that decision, she moved away from the Trails, and her son stayed…until he died. It was then that an anger so deep grew inside of her for the person who killed her son and for the streets that took him. It's for that reason that things changed after she laid eyes on her grandson for the first time. Instead of just being angry, her anger turned into war.

"Is the house cleaned out yet?"

"Yes ma'am. Cleaned out, just like I heard it was when you left."

"I don't want any neighbors," she states in her usual calm and collected manner, rarely ever having to raise her voice. Even when she's furious, she sounds as if she has no anger although the opposite is true.

"No, ma'am. I know," states the driver.

"My name is Jeneeva, not ma'am. Just because I have a grandson doesn't mean I'm old, and if there is any other person out here with that name, tell them to change it, okay? Will you do that for me?" she asks the man who responds by nodding his head to show he hears and will listen. "Now where's Kaynine?" she asks with her finger on the trigger, the gun concealed from her grandson who pays no attention to what's going on.

"She's at that girl's place...taking care of it. She'll be here. She'll be at your place soon."

"No, take me to her," she states, never trusting anything or anyone, especially on the turf that killed her husband and child. She looks over at her grandson who observes the nighttime activities, having never seen so many street walkers and children out so late at night in his entire life. Jeneeva won't hesitate to kill her grandson's own mother in order to get back what belongs to her family, so she needs to stay tied to Kaynine as closely as she can, just to make certain that she isn't trying anything other than what she was asked to do. "So you remember my son?" she asks the driver as he turns the car around.

"Yeah, sure do. Things haven't been quite right since he left here. The money has been cut, and it seems like the only thing going on was murder, taking people out that we actually needed alive, for money or for..."

"Blackmail."

"Exactly. Chief's hand was too heavy on the trigger. He just couldn't run it like..."

"Can't. Can't run it. You say it like you know he's gone. Never do that. Until he's found, until anyone is found, stay in present tense. It's time to get this place back in order, take care of everyone again."

"No problem."

"And I know he couldn't run things like my son, but trust me, there will be no more problems. Gather the girls for a head count and bring them to my new place before I get there. Get all the older ones who may know my face and the face of Kaynine. The older will teach the younger. Everything after I step out this car goes through Kaynine, understand, but I call the shots. If I change something, then I'm the law. You don't come to me ever. I call or come to you, and that goes for everyone. Make it known. We go back to the way my son delivered the money. Straighten that out so that when Kaynine sees you, it's already understood by everyone else."

"Understood."

"Come on, baby," she alerts her grandson as the car stops.

"Alright, little man," the driver states, but is cut down verbally by Jeneeva once it happens.

"This little man has a name. Look at him, Fate," she states with a smile, calling the driver by his name for the very first time. It's something that she only does if she cares enough to do so, and she remembers Fate. According to her son, he was very trustworthy and his loyalty reached to endless points across the Trails.

The driver takes another look at the child who sits there on the seat of the car while his grandmother holds his head and neck in the direction of the driver's vision. It only takes about ten seconds for him to put appearances together, but before he says a word, Jeneeva stops him.

"You got it right."

"I didn't even know," he says as a smile comes across his face like he's meeting an old friend again.

"Nobody did. I'm gonna need you to watch after him on every side. The money's good on my end. I also need you to keep quiet about it, you hear me?" He nods and she continues. "Nobody can find out, and if they do, I know who it came from. He needs to get to school and back. Your role is with him, even if I'm with him. Look out for his life before mine. His safety is your priority. It's good seeing you again, Fate. Thank you."

The driver nods, smiles back at the little boy, and then watches them walk away toward Tryina's home, already taking his assignment seriously because he knows the implications. Jeneeva is a quiet storm, the quietest he's ever seen or met in the years he has been in the streets. Even the man he knew as Bain would never cross her. She has important people outside of Gabriel's Trails on her side that no one would ever guess, and even cops were and still are on her deceased husband and son's payroll. Fate knows and understands that this is what keeps most of the head gangsters out of custody. After Bain's father passed, it was his mother who trained him the things he didn't know, but she always stayed hidden away while doing it until he implemented his own methods. Jeneeva, as everyone has already figured, was much of the brains behind the operation, so in order for Gabriel's Trails to gain what they've lost, they need her back. She is the only one that knows most of the connections that Bain died with when he stopped breathing in the trails. Outsiders who did plenty of business outside of the Trails still know her name, and they trust it but only when the business comes out of Gabriel's Trails.

As Jeneeva places her hand on the knob to open the front door, Kaynine meets her on the other side, pulling the door open from the inside of what is now a dead young lady's apartment. When she sees her son, she glances oddly at Jeneeva for bringing her son to the scene of a crime, but she quickly thwarts his entry by grabbing his hand and taking him back outside on the porch.

"Go run back to the car, baby. I'm coming. We have a new home! Aren't you excited? Now run and lay down in the back seat of the car. Your grandmother made a mistake. This isn't our house."

"Man, Ma," he pouts. "I'm sleepy. I wanna go to bed," he continues as he storms back to the car, unconcerned about any of the men standing around keeping watch in the pitch black of night. When Kaynine watches her child get back into the car and shut the door, she turns toward Jeneeva. "What was that? You can't bring him to…here!" she contests with disgust.

"I can do what I please, Kaynine. That's my grandson."

"That's my son," she states strongly. "Besides that, if shit goes down unplanned, he can't know shit."

"He doesn't know anything. Calm your voice down to me, too. It's disrespectful."

"Everything is done. She's packed up. It's gonna look right. Nobody's talking," a guy states coming from around the back of the home. He stops and takes a second glance when he sees a woman he's only seen once before in his life. He remembers her face being covered, but when she peered into the casket, she lifted her mourning along with the black veil as she stared at her only son lying there. Her face was ice cold just as her dead son's. He remembers that she didn't faint nor utter one sound, and it was the most eerie funeral he'd ever been to where a mother didn't weep for her child. That's how he remembers her face. He'd never seen anything like it. When the funeral was over, he mentioned her cold temperament to a lady named Faye who told him to keep his mouth shut because tears, no matter what the tears are for, any enemies see them as weakness. She then explained that the woman would cry later, and that she wasn't like them, not in the least, but much stronger.

"Mrs. Bain?" he hesitantly speaks, taking a couple steps back.

She hears the young man but turns her head back to Kaynine impressed. "I see you know how to keep your mouth shut," she states in regards to the man appearing to not know she was coming back to Gabriel's Trails.

"I know how to handle my business, Jeneeva," she states, subduing her frustration before adding, "and yours, too."

"In the flesh. What's your name?" Jeneeva asks the man, completely ignoring Kaynine as she is well aware that they are both in this for power and the power of their downline, therefore, although there is love, there are always conditions, especially with a woman who she can tell has always been thirsty for revenge. She is well aware of the fact that two queens are never necessary, therefore one must always call the ultimate shots. Right now, that's her, and she plans on keeping it that way until her grandson can sit them both down.

"Stacks," the guy answers.

"The money man that kept count for my son in your head? He told me good things about you, and you look just like what he said you did," she responds, noticing the missing patch of hair on the top of his head where she was told a birthmark stunted its growth. "What's the money man doing reporting back on double duty?" Jeneeva asks, believing that

Stacks should always do what he is made to do – count and keep money. From what she knows, her son's money never fell short because if it wasn't Bain watching over it, it was only one other - Stacks.

"No one else to do it right, I guess, Mrs. Bain. I remember things, photographic…all the way down to fingerprints. The house needed to be wiped down so…"

"From now on, you stick to money. That's all you do," she interjects. "Count it up, sun up to sun down. We can't get you lost in the shuffle. Certain people you protect, and one of those people is you. Getting mixed up in a murder messes everyone's money up."

Stacks stalls at her words for a second, but the second feels like one full minute because at this particular point, he feels the glare of Kaynine on him like a struck match. It's obvious that there is some friction, but how much, he doesn't know nor does he want to come in between. Therefore, he doesn't take his eyes off of Mrs. Bain when he answers, totally brushing off any stares Kaynine gives him for daring to agree with her.

"I got you. Understood. I'll get back to it."

Jeneeva smiles and then turns back to Kaynine who does nothing but watch Stacks leave. Finally, Kaynine finds it in herself to smile back at her, and when she feels the area is safe enough to speak her mind without any ears around, she does. "Undermining me isn't the way to build a stone wall, Jeneeva."

"No. You're right," Jeneeva laughs, mocking the seriousness of Kaynine. "Mine wall is built of iron."

"I put this in place for months for you, and I got it done." she snaps back through her teeth, unnerved by

Jeneeva's whole inappropriate attitude. She has never been anyone's do girl, and she's finding it difficult to be disrespected from another woman despite who she is.

"You mean *I've* been building on this for years. This is my home…our home. It's no mistake that there are no cops here yet, Kaynine. Do you really think for one second I didn't set this up, covering tracks that you, never in your wildest dreams, could?" She then lights a cigarette and blows the smoke into Kaynine's face. "I'm still alive, and that means we all are…even my son Bain."

"Yeah, I understand. I do miss him. I miss him so much," she agrees, turning away from the glaring eyes of Jeneeva to stare at the grass that shows no color because of the darkness that covers it. "But he's smiling down on us now, ma."

"He is, Kaynine…on us and his son. But now that I see what's going on over here, I need to get back to my new place so that things are running like they should run by day break. Where's the money?"

Kaynine doesn't utter another word but escorts her inside the home to show her where thousands upon thousands of dollars was once located, underneath the floor. "I got it. I got all the money. I took it out, and it's right here behind this door," she says pointing to the other room. "Nobody has gone inside. I watched it with a pistol ready as I sat on it behind the door."

Jeneeva coldly stares at her before saying, "Well, let me see."

"I took it all out myself," she assures Bain's mother.

"And you didn't let Stacks count it up?" she ponders aloud, questioning the honesty of her lesser counterpart. "Obviously, you know Stacks better than me, right?"

"I don't steal, Jeneeva."

"Sure you don't," she retorts. "Just like I don't accuse without proof. He's the money counter from here on out. That way, we always know what he have. He doesn't walk the streets, and he remains behind multiple doors…"

"That condo is still up, the one that was built up just for him. It's supplied with cameras and all."

"Well, that's his station. I do know that much. Use your phone and call him in here to get this money. Is there anymore?"

"No," Kaynine promptly responds. "If there is, she didn't tell me." As Jeneeva walks back toward the window, Kaynine's eyes stare through the walls, well aware of her lie but determined to cover it up, no matter the costs.

"Well, after he counts it, we'll see if there's any more, won't we?" she states, discounting Kaynine once again as a ploy to keep her in line psychologically. "I'm certain he still has some sort of count of what was left right inside his head. He is said to know all the earnings and can find a theft quickly."

"I'm sure he does."

"It's time to go," Jeneeva digresses, walking out of the room, leaving Kaynine in solitude pondering over everything that has transpired. It's not long before she is forced to call Stacks to have him take over the money while she follows Jeneeva to her Gabriel's Trails home.

~~

As the night passes, Javis drives. The picture of his dead mother in his mind leaves him distraught, so much so that in one instant he is sobbing uncontrollably and in another moment, he rages like a bull. Hardly no one is on the street, and as he nears Dominion Lakes, his hands begin to tremble as he remembers how he and Alexis stood in the hospital parking lot. The conversation they had didn't trigger anything in him, possibly because he was frantic about the whereabouts of his brother versus his mother at the time due to his belief that she was in a safe environment. However, as he thinks back to how she stated that she went up to his mother's room and peeped inside after he'd told her on the voicemail to wait on him in the parking lot, the question continues to bombard him on why she felt the need to get out of the car in the first place after being instructed not to do so. Why would she even peep inside at a woman who blames her for the devastation that her family has been through? As he stares at the entrance to the Dominion Lakes neighborhood, he knows the answer. It was all a cover-up for the murder of his mother for reasons he doesn't know. However, deep down to his core, he is certain she is responsible for taking the life of the only woman he's ever loved so much for all his life.

He slows down near the area where he parked Alexis' car before going into Gabriel's Trails. The car is still there, so he assumes that Alexis is there as well. He pulls up to the car and rushes out, but when he grazes against the car with his fist, completely ready to take her life with his bare hands, he notices her absence and slams his fists upon the hood of the car. From there, he places his sights on her house, and he storms toward it.

Flashbacks recreate the scene from years ago when he made this same trek to her house. Regret fills his heart as he remembers holding himself back from killing her then, but there's no stopping him now. The memory of his mother's voice calling him when he was just a youth, telling him to turn the other cheek, fails as the sight of her dead body and his brother helplessly crying for her to return to the land of the living overwhelms him. There is nowhere for his distress to be delivered except upon the living, breathing soul of Alexis. The voice of his long deceased father seems to cry out from the grave, encouraging him to leave all wrong doing, and he pauses long enough to hear him utter the Biblically clarifying words that he only tosses to the side.

"Mom's dead," he chokes out as the road blurs from his tears. "I don't want to hear what you have to say, pops. Not today. It won't be long before we are all dead, but if I kill her myself..." he continues, barely able to get anymore words out before he notices walking shadows coming out from behind Alexis' house. Immediately, he plummets to the ground, getting as flat as he can within the grass, but his eyes stay locked on the bodies as they rush off into the darkness toward Gabriel's Trails.

Breathing heavily, he focuses back on the house and then back on those who just left, obviously for the same reason he is on the way there – to kill her. Although he has that hunch, he rises in the darkness and starts his hunt once again, deciding to go behind the house just as the others. The closer he gets to the vast and dimly lit backyard, the heavier his chest feels as the magnitude of what he is about to do or what has already been done, fights to tear down all the teachings he's had as a child.

Stricken with cutting emotions, he leans against the house and begins to cry for his mother. Taking Alexis' life is the only thing left that could ease his pain, if only momentary, but in his mind, she deserves it. Everyone has paid for her wrongs but her. "Mama, I'm sorry. I'm so sorry. I was supposed to protect you. I thought I was doing the right thing. I didn't know. I thought I could get the money... Daddy. Daddy, this hurts, Pops. Oh God," he cries in puddles of despair. "She did it. I know she did it. I don't want to call the police...I can't. She's gonna get us killed, ma." His forehead rolls against the house as he finds it difficult to rip his Christian teachings from his mind. "I know I already messed up, but I thought I could... I didn't have anything else left to do, Ma! I didn't know what else to do!"

As everything around him is silent, he brushes his face off with his arm, not caring much about if he lives or dies, and continues toward the deck. From there, he moves up the stairs to become aware of the door wide open. Unafraid, he walks inside.

The place is dark, and there's absolutely no sound. Turning back around, he glances outside and makes the decision to move away from the door into a less conspicuous area of the house. Nearing the staircase, above his head he clearly sees the second floor. There is no one in sight nor are there any noises except of his own feet as they begin to climb the stairs carefully, two steps at a time. His fists are tighter than a trained fighter, and his pulse is steadier than a fair and weighted balance. Once he reaches the top, he extends his arms as if he needs to catch himself from falling, but he's really only feeling out the air, using his senses to alert him to the unexpected. That's when he peers slightly inside a room that's further down the hallway. Clearly, it's the room that belongs to Alexis. He continues to walk toward the inevitable and unpredictable before stalling in front of the bedroom door.

There are some articles of clothing strewn across the floor, but for the most part, the room appears decent and empty. He walks into the bedroom, despite all the evidence that leads him to assume she may be dead or simply not there at all. Fear has no place in him as it is completely nonexistent, especially when the first sound of footsteps against a weak floor come from the direction of a wall. He rushes over to the wall and follows the sound, and his eyes finally land at the open closet. When he stood back at the bedroom door, it looked like the closet was empty, therefore, he becomes slightly confused. He begins to move against the wall toward the closet's entrance, believing that the sound may be coming from a vent. However, when he starts to move, the footsteps he is hearing stop. For a moment, he discontinues his movement as well, but decides to keep going toward the open closet door. When he reaches the doorway, he tightens his fists and waits.

~~

She paces back and forth outside the home as the ladies get back to work on the streets. Her eyes never leave the ground, as she searches around the area for nothing except her own scrambled thoughts, which end up giving the appearance of utter confusion to the females who take glimpses back at her. Some smirk a little while others continue to tend to their business of getting money. There is one woman in particular that stands at the side of the house, right next to where Kaynine's son is sleeping as she watches Kaynine walk in circles with a pistol hanging from her hand.

Finally, instead of just standing there taking mental notes of how frail Kaynine is beginning to appear to those who don't know her, she moves in, well aware of the fact that she could get cursed out or worse than that, shot down on sight. This, however, isn't the first time she's ever had a run in with Kaynine, so she knows exactly who she's up against.

"Stop pacing," the young lady advises.

"I know you better get your ass back where you should be instead of trying to get yourself shot." Kaynine doesn't take her eyes from the ground in her response to the woman which is a callous sign of disregard and disrespect.

"Never let them see you think. Keep your thoughts private. Isn't that the way it goes?"

"Yeah," Kaynine answers, finally lifting her head at the audacity of the strange woman to think she can advise someone like her. "That is the way it goes. It makes you look like you…"

"Don't know what you're doing. Jeneeva's inside," she continues, hinting that Jeneeva is the wrong woman to show weakness.

"Mind your business."

"I've been living in Gabriel's Trails since before you left. The Trails is my business. You see those girls right there?"

"What about them?"

"They scatter, so you have to watch them closely. They're new breeds, and they think they can outsmart anyone. The fellas keep an eye on them at all times. They will head for the entrance, leave, and come back with loads of money, and no one will know a thing. Keep someone at the front and even the on the trails. They just aren't like us. They aren't loyal at all."

Kaynine rolls her eyes as she can't bear to feel like someone is kissing up, however, she decides to allow the woman to feel like she is moving up in rank. "Who are you?"

"I'm the woman you sliced."

Kaynine finally pays closer attention to the woman who claims to be the target of her past mischief. That's when she sees the scar running from the middle of her cheek to the lowest part of her earlobe. "Do you expect me to apologize?"

"No. You wouldn't do that."

"Damn right."

"I deserved it."

Kaynine smiles. "I'm glad you feel that way because your ass probably did. That taught your ass a lesson."

"I just thought I was a bad ass back then. I've changed. I know the rules."

"So why are you out of place now?" she asks, referring to her leaving the side of the house where she is to watch her son sleeping in the bedroom.

"I need something more to do, and I need more money along with it."

"Not trickin'?"

"I have HIV, so no, I'm not turning tricks. Chief and them test us every single month, saying we can't taint the network because then we'll taint the money because everyone will be sick. It wasn't until three months ago that I came up positive. So, when the girls leave out, I stay behind doing pretty much nothing, like what I'm doing now, making sure everyone's home is safe and the kids stay sleep."

Kaynine looks her over but doesn't say a word. She then checks around her shoulders to be certain no one is close enough to hear their conversation. "How long did it take my slash on your face to heal up?"

"Weeks. One of the ladies stitched it up for me, but it wasn't professionally done. That's why it bulges."

"You need to pay for meds," Kaynine repeats what she said to be certain she heard it right and to check her answer for any signs of deceit.

"Yeah, something like that. I can't make the money I used to make, and Chief wouldn't let me help with the money or selling."

"He wouldn't let you get a regular job?"

"He would, but no one ever called me. I've never worked before. Thing is, I need to stay well…even though I'm sick, you know?"

"No, I don't fuckin' know, but I understand what you're saying," Kaynine snaps, placing the female back on guard, detecting a lie in her excuse for money, so she does an even exchange. "I got your money, but it's coming in meds. You do something for me, and I'll buy that medication for you until you no longer need them."

"I'll always need them, though, Kaynine."

Kaynine goes quiet and then smiles, realizing that the woman will probably sell them for money anyway to score drugs, if her thoughts are right about her. "I'll have them for you. Just like I said. Don't leave this front door. No one comes inside, not even you. I have something to do, and whatever I do, you don't know shit about it, ever."

"Now?"

"Never a better time."

"Is it what you were thinking about?"

Kaynine raises the pistol to her head, and she freezes while Kaynine grinds her words between her teeth, "I wasn't thinking. Now, with this fuckin' gun to your head, *now*" she exclaims, "I'm thinking. I'm thinking long and hard about your ass not understanding me when I say…"

"Okay, Kaynine, I don't know what you are doing. All I do is watch the house. That's it."

"Good." She moves the gun from the woman's head, and then, she walks inside the home. Before she enters, however, she turns back to ask, "Your name again?"

"Leisure. Real name Denise."

"You don't have a real name, remember? Save that shit for your mother. You belong to me now, just like everyone else in Gabriel's Trails." She goes inside.

The house is dark. The meeting that took place here only thirty minutes ago put everyone on board with the rules that were originally implemented by Jeneeva's son. The older crew was ordered to teach the younger crew, and it was obvious as Kaynine stood next to Jeneeva that many of the older crew still looked to her as if she was Bain herself instead of just his mother. It is this fact that is enough to bother Kaynine who seethes each time she thinks about it.

She peeks inside the room where her son sleeps, and then, she walks inside the room to kiss him. He doesn't awaken. Then, she admires the room that the fellas prepared for him, like he's a king in his own castle, in a place he's never even been. He has no idea. That's when she exits the room to the sound of a shower running, shutting her son's bedroom door behind her.

Carefully, she makes it to the other room, the master bedroom. There is no sign of Jeneeva. Her bed is turned back as if she's preparing to end her night. Kaynine shakes her head and smiles at how by the word of Jeneeva needing a place to stay, her old place to stay, they implemented it at once, with no hesitation. She wants that type of power and respect. Although she has much authority still in Gabriel's Trails, much isn't good enough. She wants it all because it was ripped from her, and she's suffered from the memories of it all ever since.

"Jeneeva," she calls through the bathroom door. "I need to tell you something." When Jeneeva doesn't answer, she cracks the door. The bathroom is foggy, and she keeps the door cracked as she stands slightly outside of it against the wall. "You know back when you found out about my son, your grandchild, I'd told you that me and Bain were voluntarily together, and that I had no idea I was pregnant when I got put out of the neighborhood. I have a confession to make. I wasn't with Bain voluntarily," she admits, lifting her pistol in the air. "All that good shit I said about him, Jeneeva. The truth is, I hated your son." She steps fully inside the bathroom, and when she does, the fog starts to clear as she raises her pistol toward the shower curtain. "And he never fucking deserved his child. Sorry about this, but when you asked me to run around in the Trails and get things done so that your hands remain clean and off all the dirty money, I never intended on sharing any of it with you."

"Is that right?"

The voice strikes Kaynine's left ear from within the bedroom, but before she aims her gun from the shower curtain toward the door, she's hit with a bullet which forces her to plummet to the misty bathroom floor. Jeneeva walks inside the bathroom and takes the gun from Kaynine's hand, and while she struggles, curling herself around the hardest thing possible at the moment – the toilet – just to stay alive. Jeneeva speaks once again.

"I know he raped you. I was just thankful you decided not to throw it in my face time and time again. Made me assume that you may have been protecting my feelings as his mother. Good thing I'm not a stupid mother fucker…as you would say. I always kept it in the back of my mind that your ass was only lying to me just to set me up a for a moment like this. I know revenge is sweet. That's why I'm here standing over you right now with this gun. My revenge is immediate. Now what?"

"This," speaks another voice.

There's a blast from behind, shattering what's left of Jeneeva's life right there on the bathroom walls. The woman who shot her stands there frightened, dropping her pistol in a panic at what she's done to the Gabriel's Trails matriarch. It is then that Jeneeva takes her last long gasp before her chest completely stops moving.

"I thought I told your ass not to come in here," Kaynine struggles, as she sits up on the bathroom floor, relieved to be alive as the blood from her body covers the area around her. "I know it's you because I hear your scary ass breathing. Come help me up."

The female steps over the woman who was once the most dangerous of her time at Gabriel's Trails and goes inside the bathroom to help Kaynine from the floor. Although she had enough nerve to pull the trigger on Jeneeva, she doesn't believe she has enough stamina to swallow the pains that could come as a result of it.

"Kaynine, you have to help me. Please, you have to help me," she begs as Kaynine looks on with a smirk on her face.

215

"Doesn't it look like I'm the one who needs the mother fucking help right now? It looks like you're worrying about a dead woman, and dead people can't fight back, now can they? She got me in my arm, anyway."

"What do we do?"

"Nothing. I'm glad she shot me. It makes my job easier." Kaynine moves the female who shot Jeneeva over so that she can stand over the woman who helped take care of her son until this very day since she found out her son's blood ran through his veins. "Jeneeva, if you can still hear me. Never send a *canine* to handle your business unless you want me to take it right from under you. I have everything now, even those motherfuckers at the station that you had on payroll. I promised them more, and I got it. It's a brand new day. Rest your ass in peace. Tell Bain I said hello. Revenge is a bitch because you know what - it's not *immediate* like you said. Revenge is me. And Leisure," she speaks after retrieving her pistol from the floor.

"Yeah?" a shaken but hopeful Leisure answers.

"I told your ass to wait outside." Kaynine fires, and Leisure falls to the floor dead after being hit in the forehead. "Next time listen. Like I said, you made this so much easier to explain. This shit won't fall on me after all. Think before you shoot."

"Ma!" calls her son from the other room, obviously frightened by the noise.

"I'm coming, sweetheart. Stay in the room. Are you under the bed?"

"Yeah," he responds, his voice quivering like that of an innocent child, doing exactly as he was taught whenever he thinks he hears gunshots.

"Good. The gunshots from outside are over. Climb back in the bed. Everything is alright. Go back to sleep."

She listens for him, and when she hears him jump back on the mattress, she tends to her arm while two dead ladies lie at her feet. Meanwhile, the rich girl is backing away in fear as she becomes consumed by thoughts of who is hunting her on the other side of her bedroom wall.

~~

"Alexis? Alexis, is that you? It's me, Javis?" he calls, still tense and prepared to take the life from her lungs. However, instead of sounding threatening, he opts to outsmart her with his usual tone. "Alexis, I saw a couple guys running away from your house. If that's you inside there, come out. It's just me." With his next statement, he feels like he could crumble inside because it is far from the truth. "I need to make sure you're alright. Answer me if that's you." Finally, a voice answers.

"Javis?" her voice trembles, totally in disbelief that it's truly him. "That…it can't be you. I heard you. I heard the gunshots. They killed you!" she screams, deliberately holding the gun as tightly as she can, convinced that her mind is playing tricks on her again. "Get away from me!" she hollers. "I'll kill you! Javis is dead. You killed him! I heard it…I can still hear it," she cries, lifting one hand to her left ear. "I have a mother fucking gun, dammit!"

"No, no, Alexis. It's me. It's really me. I'm okay and alive. It wasn't me they shot. They let me go, so put the gun down. I just wanna…touch you again," he says tenderly, but full of deceit.

"Put your hand inside my closet," she blurts. "Both of them...just don't come inside. I need to make sure. I know what your hands look like. I know..."

"Here," Javis doesn't hesitate as his fists loosen, and he shows both his hands, reaching inside the closet to allow her to believe that she is safe. "See. See. It's me. I'm all alone. I promise."

"I have a gun," she cries. "You walk inside slowly. Her hands tremble atop the gun as she blinks the tears away so that she can see clearly. However, when she does clear her vision, the young man stepping in front of her isn't Javis at all, but the man she shot years ago on the trails. He's even speaking, telling her calmly to put the gun down. She's so happy to see him again, and she immediately drops the gun to run over to him and apologize for everything she's done.

Her arms are so free as she wraps her arms around him, kissing him on his warm neck and caressing his back as if she's never touched a man before. She then notices that he isn't returning the affection. Although the front of her body is warm from leaning against him, the back of her body isn't receiving the tenderness of warm hands as she believes it should. Not understanding why there is no reciprocation for her love, she slowly moves her hands from his body, and his skin tone changes before her very eyes. Bound by a fit of confusion, she glances back at his face to notice he's staring right back at her.

"My mother's dead."

"Javis..." she states, still happy to see him but oblivious to his words, realizing fairly quickly that she's temporarily lost her mind and that the man standing before her isn't happy. In the seconds it takes for her to regain her senses, she comes to grips with the pain and rage in his face, and she understands that he must know.

"And you killed her." His fists close once again, and just as the tremors in his neck buckle under the pressure of his rage, his veins warp beneath his skin, revealing the ultimate danger facing her.

She lifts her hands to add space between them. "No…no…I saw her, and I apologized, but she…Javis, no," she begs before breaking from her stance to reach back and grab the gun that she left on the floor only two feet away. Before she can even take hold of it, Javis grabs her by her hair and throws her backwards against the closet wall. When she goes for the pistol again, Javis has already reached for it, aiming directly at her.

"It was always you."

"Wait, Javis, wait! I didn't mean to hurt her," she pleads, forcefully pulling clothing from off the hangers and shoving them in front of her as if the flimsy make of cotton and silk can intercept the bullet that is aiming right for her chest. "Javis, stop it. Don't!"

"My mom would suffer through a lot of things, Alexis, but she would never take her own life. She was a proud woman. She was my mother," he hollers as Alexis screams for her life, regretting everything up to this point, but it's too late. Javis pulls the trigger, leaving her body gasping for air up against the clothing that she pulled down around her at the doorway.

Tears fall from his face, and he releases the pistol because suddenly, all of his rage is replaced by an unsettling question – what happens next? The voices of his mother and father shout behind him, *"Don't do this anymore. We are still gone, son. Vengeance is the Lord's. You're not a murderer, child. Leave."*

As he panics, realizing the totality of what he has done, placing not only himself at risk for being caught but placing his only sibling left to fend for himself, he realizes that he needs to get the money for his brother just in case. Therefore, he checks Alexis' pockets as she continues to pull at his shirt. He shoves her off, and she hits the floor again, then he finds what he's searching for. The car keys. As he runs out, he leaves her there to die at her closet door.

Taking the staircase like he's in a track meet, he bolts through the house and out the backdoor from where he entered, leaving everything as it was when he saw it, except the bloody mess upstairs. His mind is focused on the bag, the one thing that he knows she packed that was inside her car. It must be the money. It has to be.

The night chases him no matter how fast he runs behind the homes until he reaches Alexis' car. Before he makes a move toward the driver's side door, he stalls to make certain no one is around. His heart races, but the only thing he must do is get his hands on the money to secure his brother's future in case his own future is taken away. When he is sure no one is around, he makes a run for the car and tries various keys until he gets inside, his hands nervously fidgeting. He's about to sit, but then decides not to do so, realizing that it may somehow leave evidence behind of what he's done. Then, he spots the bag. Quickly, he leans over, trying his hardest not to touch anything else in the car. When he takes hold of it, he tosses the bag out of the car. Opening it reveals that there are clothes inside, and as he continues to shuffle things around, there is money, more than what he may need from what his eyes can count. Needing to wipe down the car, he removes one of Alexis' shirts and begins to clean the steering wheel and even wipe the leather seats, including the outside of the car. From there, he takes the keys, wipes them off as well, and then drops them onto the ground. His car is right there next to hers, so it's not long before he removes himself from the scene of what will end up being the main link to the second murder to occur in Dominion Lakes in days.

Speeding down the road, he backtracks every step he's ever taken from the time he's met Alexis. Relief spills through the pores on his skin in the form of sweat as he rolls down every window in the car in hopes to dry off. Every red light that causes him to stop creates a tunnel of paranoia as he grows certain that he will be caught before hiding the money in his home for his brother. Therefore, in a split second, he changes his route and heads back to the hospital, having to stop only for gas that he purchases with the stolen money.

"I need to get him. I need him... Mama...I'm gonna protect him. He's gonna be fine," he babbles like a young man going out of his mind from the pressures of life that have left him no choice but to run away. "I'm sorry!" The scream is so loud until the driver of the car that rides beside him glances over to see a pitiful young man with tears streaming down his face under the lit street. As the driver slows, clearly disturbed at what he sees, he allows Javis to continue on down the road as he follows him on a path that leads directly to the hospital. When Javis pulls into the parking lot, the man follows closely behind as Javis is oblivious to him. However, when Javis exits his car befuddled and seriously confused, he is taken by surprise when he notices a man walking toward him, reaching for his arm.

"Son."

"Get off me, man! Who are you?" Javis responds, swinging his fist, barely missing the man whom he can barely recognize through the sheet of unrelenting tears in his eyes.

The aged man backs away with his hands open and in the air. "It's me, Javis. It's your pastor. Your brother called me, said your mom had me listed in the records, and I came right up. Passed you on the highway, son. I'm sorry."

"Pastor Cloven?" After stating his pastor's name, just as if he is still a juvenile boy, he falls into his pastor's arms and then to the ground, his pastor kneeling down to the hard, black street with him.

"It's good to see you again, son. I'm sorry it had to be under these circumstances. I'm here. I may not be over the church anymore, but I'm right here with you, not going anywhere. Believe you me, I'm here."

Javis grips his shirt and moans three words twice, "It's too late. It's too late." His tears soak through his pastor's shirt as his pastor begins to pray, unaware that the young man he consoles is in over his head from more than just the death of his mother and mounting debt. They both rise from the street and go inside the hospital before his mother is moved to the morgue.

~~

"Help me," she whimpers as she crawls to the round rug in the center of her bedroom with her pistol in her hand that Javis dropped to the floor before he ran from her house. There's a stream of blood that flows from her body to the closet where she was shot, but not enough blood has left her system to cause her heart to completely stop. "Mama," she begs softly for her mother to come and hold her head as she used to do when she was just a small child. All the pain would just go away, and this is what Alexis wants right now but can't get.

Her landline phone is adjacent to the headboard of her bed. She can barely reach it, but once she pulls herself again, she is able to knock it off the standing charger with her finger. The phone collapses onto its side, and she begins to dial, not emergency, but her mother. At first, there's no answer, however, after the third ring, her mother picks up.

"Hello, hello, Lexis, baby? Baby, are you there? Lex?"

"Mama…"

"What's wrong? Tell me. You're at home. Michael, she's at the house. I'm turning around. Alexis, I'm on my way, just what's wrong?"

"I'm shot, Mama," Deep exhales and inhales penetrate the phone like knives through her mother's heart as Alexis continues to gasp out more words. "I'm gonna die. Just leave me. I love you, but I've been waiting for this."

"Lexi? Lexis!" she screams through the phone, releasing the steering wheel at fifty-five miles an hour, causing her husband to snatch the wheel and force a stop in the middle of the road. Throwing on the brake, he grabs her shoulders as she hollers into the phone.

"What, Lorah, what? What is it?"

"Our baby…she's just killed herself, Michael. She's just died!"

He seizes the cell phone from her hands, puts it to his ear and shouts, "Alexis, answer me! Answer me, dammit!"

On the other end of the phone, Alexis lies lifelessly on the floor of her bedroom until the sound of her parents' voices are no more.

~~

The very next day that comes around, Jeneeva is found by police. She is shot, lying face down in her home that's located outside of Gabriel's Trails. As the detective combs the scene, he walks into the middle of the street, away from the house and makes a phone call.

"It's done."

"Your money will be at the drop. It's a new day. A brand new day." She ends the call and sends her son out to school, this time chauffeured by no one other than the man named Fate who basically drove Jeneeva to her own death. As she smiles and waves good-bye to her son like everything is normal while her arm remains covered and stitched up, away from the innocent eyes of her son. The smile quickly fades as the gangsters and prostitutes approach her, walking toward her home from each direction of the trails. She stares back at them with a clear conscience and whispers to herself with a smirk. "Yeah, it's my Trails now."

THE END

Thank you for reading the **Gabriel's Trails** series, from **Murders at Gabriel's Trails** to **Sins of Bain** and **Deception at Gabriel's Trails**.

Continue to follow The Gabriel's Trails series at mirikacornelius.com for updates and upcoming stories in the series.

READ MORE AKIRIM PRESS BOOKS

Books by Mirika Mayo Cornelius

(mirikacornelius.com)

The Secret Novel Collection

Ain't Quite What I Thought!

Ain't Quite What I Thought! 2

First Degree Sins

Cold Blooded Goons

Inside the Gates of Doons

Sunny Sides of My Shade

Murders at Gabriel's Trails: The Complete 5 Part Series plus bonus Sins of Bain

Deception at Gabriel's Trails: The Complete Series

I Thought I Was Alone Trilogy

Most Wanted Felon

Curse the Cotton

Disguised by a Raging Smile

Books by Rod Cornelius

(rodcornelius.com)

Ugly

Single Again

Diggin' Gold

The Trusted

Ghetto Eyes

The Best Kept Secrets

Whatever It Takes

Books by Cyan Deane

(mirikacornelius.com/cyan-deane)

Dead Man's Mayhem

Execution's Karma